A Pointed End
Kit McKenna

McKenna Publishing, LLC

Other Books By Kit McKenna

THE OKLAHOMA SKIES SERIES

All Sorrows Are Less

https://mybook.to/AllSorrowsKitMcKenna

Paint the Earth Red

https://mybook.to/PaintEarthKitMcKenna

The Heart That Returns

https://mybook.to/HeartReturnsKitMcKenna

Perfect As You Are

https://mybook.to/PerfectKitMcKenna

The Art of Passion

https://mybook.to/ArtPassionKitMcKenna

A Matter of Trust

https://mybook.to/MatterTrustKitMcKenna

Get a FREE copy of the Valentine Short Mr. Wrong door

https://dl.bookfunnel.com/myptwbvjh0

THE BELLADONNA SOCIETY SERIES

A Pointed End

https://mybook.to/PointedKitMcKenna

A Murderous Intent

https://mybook.to/MurderousKitMcKenna

A Secret Revealed

https://mybook.to/RevealedKitMcKenna

A Devil's Snare

https://mybook.to/SnareKitMcKenna

A Predator's Threat

https://mybook.to/ThreatKitMcKenna

THE MORRIGAN MAFIA SERIES

Crossed

https://mybook.to/CrossedMcKenna

Coup

https://mybook.to/CoupKitMcKenna

Crashed

https://mybook.to/CrashedKitMcKenna

Control

https://mybook.to/ControlKitMcKenna

Trigger Warning

This book contains instances of domestic abuse that may be triggering to survivors.

Prologue

N oémie

 1975 Hugo, Oklahoma

"Your aunt wasn't with us long, but she sure was a popular attraction while she was. She traveled light except for the machine. It will be a monster to move by yourself," Mr. Miller tells me before he tilts up the bottle of Mr. Pibb to take a drink.

His clothing, chinos topped by a button-down shirt and cardigan against the chilly air, is a couple of years behind the fashion trends. However, although they aren't top of the line, they're good quality, which means his show must do fairly well.

"I have hired a truck service to take it to Oklahoma City for me," I tell the man.

"That's smart," he says, studying me with a practiced eye. "You got the same Frenchie accent she had," he observes. "The cake eaters ate it up."

"Oui, I came from France when the news of her death reached me."

Truthfully, I sold everything I had to finance the journey. I have enough left to pay for the move to Oklahoma City and a bit left over to fund lodgings for a short time. However, the journey to retrieve the machine will be more than worth it.

"You know, you could take over her spot. I know this life isn't for everyone, but we have a good crew here. Better than most. We're clean and we don't allow a lot of the nonsense that goes on with other outfits."

"I greatly appreciate the offer; it is truly tempting, but I have an arrangement in Oklahoma City awaiting me," I reply. Thinking I might keep an open door just in case I need it, I add, "However, should that not work out, I will seek you out to see if you are still amenable to having me join your troupe."

"Well, that's just my bad luck. But yeah, keep us in mind. We'd love to have someone such as yourself for our show."

Mr. Miller is one of those rarest of creatures, a man who's hard to read. I can't tell if he knows I'm lying or if he truly believes what I've told him. It also isn't clear what he means by someone such as myself.

Perhaps he means a French woman or he may know my aunt and I are of the Romani people. If the latter, he is a rare creature, indeed. Most people hold our ilk in contempt. To be a gitan, a gypsy, in much of the world, is as good as being trash and less than human.

Some people I do not know declared a few years ago that we should no longer call ourselves gypsies. Instead, we're supposed to call ourselves Romani. but a lifetime of identifying as a gitan is difficult to overcome for me. Even more so for my family who have been gitan in southern France for hundreds of years.

We kept our true ethnicity a secret, of course, lest we end up branded, or worse. Throughout history, my people have been persecuted. Sometimes cast out, but often murdered outright in massive numbers. The need to keep our secrets is partly what led to me being here now.

If Mr. Miller knew what he had in my aunt's belongings, he would forget about me and surely cut my throat to keep it for himself. I'm saved from further conversation by the truck that comes bouncing down the rough road.

I hope he has enough rope and padding to secure everything to avoid damage. That would be a shame if I had come all this way only to have the machine bounced to pieces on these horrible roads.

"This won't take care of the whole of the bill for the move, most likely, but it should help. These are the wages that were due your aunt when she passed." He hands me an envelope. I flip it open to see that it's cash instead of a check, then close it and slide it into my purse.

"Thank you. I greatly appreciate it."

I'm surprised and touched by the gesture. If he had said he had to keep any wages due to her to cover the cost of storing her possessions, it would have been much less surprising. I have no idea how much it is or if it's everything she was owed, but the fact that he gave me any part of her outstanding wages raises my estimation of the veracity of his statements about his traveling troupe being better than most.

The driver, all wiry muscle and bone, parks the truck and swings down from the cab and looks at a piece of paper on a clipboard. "Imma lookin' fer a Nayomee Theory."

"Se moi," I reply and hold up my hand. I don't bother to correct his pronunciation of my name; there's no point in it.

Mr. Miller kindly asks two of his men to assist the trucker with getting the machine and few other bits loaded. My arrangement is to ride to Oklahoma City in the truck with him. Although it might not be the most comfortable ride, this will save me the cost of bus fare when all my coins are dear.

Predictably, when we are about halfway into the time I was given for the trip, we stop for gas and the driver makes a proposal. Out of the corner of my eye, I've watched him ogling my legs and I must admit, I purposely let a little more show than was needed.

Thankfully, he's a decent-looking man. He was probably quite handsome when he was young. Even in middle age, he is still fit and easy enough on the eyes.

There are positives and negatives to an ugly man, though. Although the view isn't pretty, you can always close your eyes and they're typically more grateful, which means they're often more generous. As long as they're clean, I don't much care.

Once the tanks are full, he pulls into a mostly empty rest area and parks in the back to afford some privacy. I ignore the wedding ring on his left hand, give him the best ten-minute ride of his life, and he gives me a fifty percent discount on the freight cost. I was hoping for free, but the unexpected money

Mr. Miller gave me had me feeling more attuned to getting to our destination than haggling over a discount.

For the rest of our ride, I review the information sent to me by my aunt. Although she'd been with the circus for a few years, she had bigger plans. When she started feeling ill, she passed along her plans and the supporting information to me so that it might not go to waste.

I would never have thought that some small backward area of the United States called Oklahoma would have the potential she was predicting it was on the verge of. However, when I reviewed the information she sent me, I had to admit I could see it, too.

It would have been best if her plans had been instigated a year ago, maybe two. Her illness prevented it, though, and I was not ready yet. When she wrote to me three years ago, I started saving every penny I could.

I study the photos in the newspaper clippings even though I've already spent hours memorizing every one. There are three that I have chosen as prime candidates, so now, it's just a matter of discovering where they'll be, and when, so that I might arrange an introductory encounter.

A couple of hours later, I put my papers away as we arrive at our destination where we are met by my future landlord, an older man with a kindly face. In our communication, he told me he was a widower, and it shows in his slightly off-kilter appearance. His shirt is rumpled and his entire ensemble is mismatched.

The driver unloads everything into the small apartment I made arrangements to lease before I started my journey. I thank him, pay him the discounted funds he is due, and close the door on the past, ready to start a new future.

Chapter 1

Caitlyn

My baby walks across the stage and I don't know if I should cry or clap. I settle on both. She might be old enough to walk into any bar and order alcohol now, but Margaret Foster will always be my baby.

When I look over at her father, he has tears in his eyes, too. Regardless of how he treated me, he was always a good father to Maggie, so I can't begrudge his pride in her accomplishment.

Once the ceremony ends, we wait for her at the designated location. Benjamin keeps checking his watch. For some reason, he thinks I'm oblivious, but I know full well why he's in a hurry.

"Daddy! Mom!" Maggie is racing toward us, her cap askew and gown trailing behind her. She races into Benjamin's arms and he lifts her off the ground. He used to swing her around, but that might give him a heart attack these days.

"Congratulations, baby," I tell her when she turns her attention to me. Pulling her into a hug, I tell her, "I'm so proud of you."

We spend some time taking the obligatory graduation photos, but soon, it's both Maggie and her father checking their watches. "Listen," I finally say, "I know you probably have a million things to do. Are we still on for dinner?"

"Yes, of course. Seven o'clock, right?"

"Right. That way you will be done in time for any parties you need to go to," I confirm with a grin.

"Thanks, Mama. I love you." With one last hug for each of us, she races off again.

We watch her go until she disappears into the crowd. "Well, I guess I'll see you at dinner tonight," Benjamin says, evaporating every bit of happiness I have in this moment.

"Yes, and Benjamin," I wait for him to turn to me and pay attention because I don't want any misunderstanding. "I will be checking out tomorrow morning for both rooms. You said you want to spend some time here in Boston, but I will not be footing the bill for you and your girlfriend's vacation."

His attempt to act shocked falls short. "What do you mean?"

"I know you still think of me as the nineteen-year-old idiot you married, but she's been gone a long time. You and your girlfriend couldn't have been more obvious at breakfast this morning."

He stands there gaping at me, so I go on.

"Is she even old enough to drink? Oh wait, it doesn't matter. She can't drink anyway because she's what? Five months pregnant? Or is it six? Never mind, I don't care."

Certain I've made myself clear and let him know exactly how not fooled I am, I turn on my heel and walk away. There's just enough time for me to make my spa appointment and goodness knows I need it.

Watching Benjamin and his latest mistress skulking around for the past few days has been equal parts humorous and frustrating. He was supposed to be coming here for our daughter's college graduation, not taking a vacation with his latest. However, I guess the temptation to get at least a portion of the trip paid for by me was too much to resist.

I'm feeling as loose as cooked spaghetti when I return to my room with just enough time to get ready for dinner. The massage therapist tracked down every knot of tension like a bloodhound and pulverized it to goo. Just as I'm stepping onto the elevator, Maggie calls out, "Mama!"

When I turn, I see she's already dressed for dinner. "Hi, darling! You're early."

She hooks her arm in mine as we wait for the elevator to return. "Yeah, I wanted to talk to you since I know you're flying back home in the morning."

"All right. What's up?"

"Let's wait until we get to your room. Oh, your toes look pretty."

I wiggle my newly painted piggies. "Thank you. I decided to end my obsession with beige nails."

"That's an excellent decision."

During the ride up the elevator, she tells me about spending the afternoon with her sorority sisters and the very important rites of passage that had to be completed. Senior sisters made a production of passing on the keys of the kingdom to the incoming leadership and what not.

Once we're closed in my hotel room, I leave my water bottle and room key on the table and settle into a chair. "What's up?"

She doesn't mince words. "I saw Daddy with another woman today. He doesn't know I saw him, though."

I sigh. It's exactly what I hoped wouldn't happen when I realized he'd brought his mistress with him.

"You knew?" she asks, her voice colored with shock.

On some level, I hoped she would never know her father was anything but perfect. However, she's an adult now and I won't lie to her.

"Yes. He started having affairs soon after we were married. We haven't been together as husband and wife since I became pregnant with you."

She stares at me for long moments. "Why did you stay with him?"

She doesn't need to know all the dynamics at play in my relationship with her father. In a daughter's eyes, their father is a god. They have a close, loving relationship and I don't want to damage that.

"Because of you and your brothers. Other than cheating, he was never cruel to me, so it was easy to let him be him while not disrupting your home life. I know it's a shock, but your father has always loved you and I don't want to demean him to you. It's okay to love him as you always have. Let me wash off the massage oil quickly, then we can chat while I dress."

I shower as quickly as I can, not wanting to keep her waiting. When I emerge from the bathroom in a robe, Maggie is seated in a chair by the window, staring out at the city below.

I pull on my undergarments, then slip back into my robe to put on makeup at the vanity.

"As you know," Maggie says, "I've been working part time for the company I interned with last summer. They've liked my work and have offered me a full-time position here in Boston .""Oh, darling, that's wonderful! I know that's what you were hoping for."

"One of my sorority sisters has been offered a position in town, too, and we've talked about getting an apartment together. Um, Boston is expensive, so I might need some help to get settled."

"Don't let that worry you. I'll help you however you need."

"Thanks, Mama. I really appreciate it." She turns and levels troubled eyes at me. "So, since I'm staying here and the boys are in Colorado and California, you don't have to worry about our home life anymore."

I cross the room to her and put a hand to her cheek. "Maggie, I don't want you to worry about me and your dad, but I appreciate the sentiment. I've been thinking about downsizing since it's only me in the house most of the time, so it's good to know you'll be fine with that."

She shivers. "I never liked our house. The kids at school used to tell me it was haunted."

I laugh. "Seriously?"

"Yeah. That's why I never would stay there alone. If there was a chance of it, I would find a friend's house to go hang out at until someone else would be there."

"Oh, honey, I wish you'd told me!"

She shrugs. "It's all over and done now. But yeah, I'd love to never have to go there again."

Not a lot of time is spent on make-up and hair. I need to be presentable for the venue, but there's no one to impress, so it doesn't take me long to get ready. Maybe Benjamin won't show up and it will be just Maggie and me.

One can hope, anyway.

Chapter 2

Ford

"Dalton! You're going the wrong way!" I yell across the field.

The kid is so excited about having the ball and a clear path to the goal line that he's blocking out everything else. For the love of God, someone needs to tag him. He'll never get over it if he crosses the wrong goal line.

"I'm going to kill him," my brother, Al, growls next to me.

"You can't do that. He's only eight," I retort with a chuckle. "Besides, I'd never live down having to arrest my own brother."

From the corner of my eye, I see the streak of a red and black jersey. Shamika Davis is sailing past everyone. Go, girl.

Dalton looks over his shoulder and tries to speed up when he sees her coming, but it's no use. Shamika is the fastest person on the team. She's almost in range to grab his flag when Dalton trips and goes down.

The ball pops out in a fumble. All the other players are completely confused about what's going on, so they're meandering around in mid-field, unsure what to do. Shamika blazes past Dalton, grabs the ball, does an about face and takes off toward the goal line. The correct goal line.

She's cruising down the field when a big boy on the other team gets a clue and meets her head on. They go down in a tangle of limbs at about the thirty-yard line with the big kid's hand wrapped firmly around her face mask and yellow flags fly from pretty much every ref on the field.

Although the penalty was obvious, I think it took them a while to stop laughing at the play that led to it. Tackling is strictly prohibited in kid's football these days, but a facemask has always been a penalty and the refs take it seriously. The kid who did it will not only earn a penalty for his team, but in this league, he's also benched for the rest of the quarter.

"Bonnie wants to know if you're coming to Sunday lunch," Al says.

"Give her my usual answer. I'll be there if I'm not working."

"Are you ever going to retire?"

"Someday."

Some days I want to hand in my notice ASAP. Other days, I can't imagine leaving the police force. The first usually happens when I work on a particularly heinous case. The other when I put the bastard in jail with enough evidence for a slam dunk conviction.

Although being a homicide detective can wear a person down, there's no better feeling than when I take another criminal off the streets.

"You need to retire and get a job that lets you have a life."

"I have a life."

"No, you don't. You work, and that's about it."

"What's wrong with that if I like it? Besides, I'm not working now, am I?"

I shouldn't have said it. Uttering a sentence like that is the ultimate invitation for fate to step in and stir the pot.

The refs on the field finally mete out the penalty. Shamika's progress has another fifteen yards added to it, and that puts us in range for a quick touchdown and four downs to do it. Al signals a play and the kids take their places in the formation.

My phone buzzes in my pocket. Al gives me some side eye, able to hear the buzz even above the noise from the kids and the parents in the stands. When I check the screen, sure enough, it's work.

Al knows the routine, so he's not surprised when I step away behind the bleachers to take the call. I return and don't even have to tell him that I'm getting called in. He's holding out a hand to me.

I take it in mine and he pulls me close, his other hand going around to clap me on the back in the manly hug that guys do. "Love you," he says. "Stay safe."

"You know it," I reply. "Love you, too. Tell Bonnie I'll try and make it Sunday."

Making a beeline to my car, I open the back door and take off my black and red team jacket so I can put on a suit coat. I always keep one on a hanger dangling from the oh shit handle behind the driver's seat.

Twenty minutes later, I'm pulling to the curb in front of a small house with more than a few cop cars to signal I'm in the right spot. There is a crowd of people standing outside the yellow tape, an older woman bawling her eyes out, flanked by two other women.

I can see someone in the back seat of a patrol car. It's probably the suspect, but I'll find out for sure when I check in.

With every step up the driveway, the mantle of homicide detective falls over my shoulders. My emotions are shut off, and ice fills my blood. When I go through the door, I almost fall to my knees.

"What do we have, Mickey?" I ask the uniform at the door.

"It's bad, Detective."

"I see that. The guy in the car the doer?"

"Yeah. Admitted it outright."

I watch the forensics team work for a moment because the urge to walk out to the car and put a bullet in the guy's head is strong and I need to cool off. Instead of asking Mickey the reason, I'll wait until I get the guy down to the station and in an interrogation room.

My partner Jim Bergen steps through the front door. "Holy shit," he says low.

"Yeah. Mickey, whose car is that the perp's in?"

"Johnson's," Mickey answers.

"Thanks. Jim, forensics is going to be here a while. What do you say we follow Johnson to the station and interview the husband?"

Jim's hand makes scratching noises as he rubs it over his stubbly jaw. "Yeah."

When I step outside, I take a deep breath, trying to clear the smell of sour blood out of my head. Most people can't smell blood when it's freshly spilled unless it's in quantity. I'm one of the rare people that can.

Blood that's a few hours old smells rancid to me, even in small amounts. The amount of blood spread over this crime scene looks like Mr. Williams emptied every drop from his wife and infant son. What makes a man do such a thing?

Two hours later, I have my answer. The baby had colic and Mr. Williams "just needed to get some sleep." His answer to the incessant crying was to beat his son to death and then his wife when she tried to stop him.

He proceeded to go back to bed to get his much needed sleep. That's exactly where the officers found him when they arrived after being called by the neighbors who heard the screaming.

Chapter 3

Caitlyn

As I sit across the breakfast table from Benjamin, I find myself wishing he would die and release me from this interminable farce of a marriage. He is sitting there slurping up his oatmeal like he doesn't have a care in the world. But then, he doesn't, does he?

Even now, as he takes a piece of toast from the rack on the table and begins buttering it, I think of climbing over the breakfast dishes, taking the knife out of his hand, and stabbing it into his gut. I have heard that a stabbing to the abdominals is a horribly painful way to die, particularly if I could manage to perforate his intestines.

However, I'm not sure if the knife would do any real damage. It is just a butter knife, so it's not very sharp. Plus, the amount of flab Ben has accumulated around his gut in recent years might not even allow the knife to reach as far as his intestines.

How on earth does he convince women to sleep with him? It must be the money. I wonder what would happen if he was forced to live within the salary provided by his job. Would he still be able to get those young women to sleep with him if he wasn't spending a bunch of money on them? Hopefully, we'll find out soon enough.

Letting my eyes roam his body, I wonder if maybe I could jab the knife into the side of his neck. Hitting the jugular couldn't be that difficult, could it? Either way, it would make a terrible mess and there would be the body to dispose of.

Not to mention that I'd go to prison, too. No, there is no helping it. I simply cannot stab Benjamin in the gut or the throat at the moment.

Damn practicality.

Ben stops mid-slather. "Cait?"

I blink and look up to see him staring at me wide-eyed. "Yes?"

"Are you okay? You have the strangest look on your face."

"Oh, I'm fine. I was just thinking about something."

"Well, from the look on your face, it looked like you were ready to disembowel me."

I smile sweetly.

Goddamn right, I'm ready to. Have been for about twenty-five years. I really don't want him dead, I just want him to go away. Now that I know Maggie is staying in Boston, there's no reason to maintain the façade any longer and as soon as I got home after her graduation, I came up with a plan and started taking steps.

She was right; with the boys out west and her staying put where she is, the stasis bubble can be broken. Finally, I can take charge of my life and start living it on my terms.

I get up to take my plate to the kitchen and look him in the eyes as I stand. "Maybe I was. Excuse me," I say as I put my back to the swinging door that leads to the kitchen and push through.

I have to get out of this room before I throw up all over the table and certainly before I lose it, and decide to give the butter knife a go. As I make my way upstairs to dress for the day, I run my fingers over the dark wood paneling.

I hate this place.

The décor is so dark and dreary that even with a ten thousand square foot floor plan, it feels claustrophobic and depressing. I imagine the builder was thinking about grand English estate homes when it was built, but he fell far short of the charm he likely intended. No wonder Maggie's friends told her the place was haunted.

My preferences always leaned toward open spaces and lots of light, essentially the exact opposite of this tomb. The house was to my father's taste. If nothing else, my father probably liked it because it was one of the largest homes in our neighborhood.

He always was one who liked to be ostentatious. It was sort of a wedding gift from him, and we had been appreciative at the time, but the wedding that tied me to Benjamin was long ago, and my father is dead and gone. We hadn't been given title to the place, only allowed to live here.

It was just like dear old dad to give gifts that were either a backhanded insult or replete with strings. It's time to sell. If he doesn't like me getting rid of this enormous monstrosity, he can take it up with Saint Pete or Lucifer, whichever being is the overlord of his afterlife domain.

In my room, I play with my hair, trying to decide if I should pin it back or wear it down. A few days ago, I had a moment where I thought about coloring my ash blonde hair to cover up the strands of silver I am seeing more of these days. However, I simply couldn't bring myself to do it. Growing older is a natural part of life.

Besides, it's not like there is a man around to look younger for. God knows Ben's attention is elsewhere. Not that I want his attention anymore. There is just me and I don't mind.

I keep in good shape because it makes me feel healthy and strong, not because there is anyone to see me naked. The way I look is pretty good, if I do say so myself, even if I am a little rounder than I was twenty-five years ago. Having three children will do that to a body.

I let out a sigh.

It takes me some time to get dressed. I want to make a good impression. I'm not sure why, though. After all, I am the one paying. They should be the ones trying to make a good impression on me. Still, I want to get it just right; I want to appear confident and capable.

Quit dilly dallying and get dressed. You've got your entire future ahead of you.

Chapter 4

Caitlyn

S top fidgeting and look at the pictures on the wall or something.

It would have been better if they'd left me in the lobby. At least I could have people watched there. Unfortunately, I'm in a waiting room...waiting. Frosted glass walls are closed in with locked frosted glass doors on either side, so it feels a bit more like a holding pen than a comfortable rest area.

The artwork on the walls is atrocious and therefore my study of it doesn't provide much of a distraction. I shift in my seat again. The chairs look prettier than the art, but they are horribly uncomfortable. Needing to move, I stand.

I stroll around the small room in a circular motion instead of back and forth. Not wanting to appear as if I am pacing impatiently, I measure my steps and take my time. I am impatient, but I don't want it to look that way. With this being a law firm, they probably have cameras everywhere.

It's my fault that I have time to burn, which allows my impatience to fester. I'm the one who showed up a few minutes early as I always do, so I will have to wait as I am accustomed to.

"Mrs. Foster?"

I look up at the mention of my name to see a sharply dressed young man. His shiny gray suit and funky tie are out of the ordinary in this neck of the woods. He's way trendier than most native Okies. He has sharp eyes to go with his sharp clothes and we study each other for a breath.

"Yes," I confirm.

"Hello, I'm Simon Jones, Ms. Hartman's associate. I'll show you to the conference room."

"Thank you." I follow Simon down a hall until he pauses and opens a frosted door for me to enter a room behind another frosted glass wall.

"Ms. Hartman will be right in. May I offer you some coffee or water?"

My throat dry, I accept his offer of water. I don't feel nervous or anxious exactly. If anything, I'm hopeful. Hopeful that the fresh eyes of a new attorney will bring fresh results.

Simon exits the room, leaving me alone in a small conference room with a round table and four chairs that, upon taking a seat, I discover aren't any more comfortable than those in the waiting area. This room is also quite austere. There certainly aren't any client dollars being invested into the firm's décor.

Exactly at our appointment time, Andrea Hartman breezes into the room with Simon in tow. "Mrs. Foster, I apologize for the wait." She puts her things down with a thump and comes around the table to shake my hand. "It's a pleasure to meet you."

"Please, call me Cait." My initial gut reaction to this woman is that I like her. She has a firm handshake and makes eye contact.

The last attorney I had spoken with, stodgy old Mr. Johnson of the firm my father had used for years, couldn't even bring himself to look me in the eye.

I was never sure if it was the discrepancy in our ages or genders. Perhaps he had been regaled by my father of my shortcomings often enough that his view of me was tainted. Perhaps, like my father, he couldn't forgive me for not being a son to carry on with my father's legacy, either.

By contrast, Ms. Andrea Hartman, alleged family law phenom, is warm and confident. Her eyes are intelligent and kind. She is polished and professional in Prada with the demeanor of a warrior. I hope her demeanor holds true in reality. A warrioress or even a goddamn Valkyrie is exactly what I need to slay some dragons on my behalf.

"I think we'll get right into things, Cait. I've looked over the documents you sent, along with the information from your private investigator. The prenuptial agreement was drawn up by your father, correct?"

"Yes."

"He would not allow you to marry without the agreement, correct?"

"Yes," I confirm.

"There is some precedent in case law that I'd like to see if we can exploit. It is typically used when one spouse is more financially savvy than the other. In those cases, if one prospective spouse is considered less sophisticated than the other in financial issues, and this person was placed under pressure or threat to sign such an agreement, the court may set aside the prenup."

She draws out another sheet of paper from under the one on top, then continues. "Although there was not a great differentiation in your financial knowledge at the time between you and your husband, it could be said that you were pressured or coerced to sign the agreement by your father. You were only nineteen at the time, correct?"

"Yes, I had just turned nineteen a few weeks before we were married."

"And your husband was…"

"He was twenty-four. We met while I was a freshman at the University of Oklahoma and Benjamin was a senior."

She raises an eyebrow and makes a note of it. "There is another potential avenue we can make use of. Your husband's latest mistress is pregnant, correct?"

I sigh. "Yes, she's due in three months."

"So, your husband is obviously having unprotected sex. Have you had sex with him recently?"

I knew this topic was likely to come up, but it still makes me uncomfortable.

"No. I haven't had sex with him since I became pregnant with our daughter over twenty years ago. He started having affairs just a few weeks into our marriage, but I was heavily influenced by my father who, although he didn't approve of Benjamin's philandering, believed that the man was the head of the household and if my husband was having an affair, it was because I wasn't properly fulfilling my wifely duties. My father passed away a few months into my third pregnancy and that's when I stopped having sex with my husband."

According to the private detective I hired as soon as I returned from Boston, Benjamin's latest is only six months older than our daughter. I do not know the number of women there had been between the first and this latest, but I have no doubt there are many. Benjamin always has had a short attention span that benefited from his ability to be extremely charming.

"Have any of his other mistresses become pregnant?"

"Not that I'm aware of."

"There is also a precedence that unprotected sex with others while still sleeping with you could be used as a basis for criminal negligence in that he could pass along sexually transmitted diseases. However, there would be no way to prove that his sexual relations were unprotected at that time unless you have specific names of individuals that we might track down and depose."

"I do not." I sigh again.

Why the hell didn't you pay more attention when you were younger?

"On the other matters, there is nothing in the prenup or trust that requires you to provide him with additional monthly financial support above his own earnings."

She moves her papers around again. "Also, the house is part of the trust and is subject to the prenup as an asset. If you sell, the proceeds revert to the trust. If you purchase new and pay using funds from the trust, it will also become an asset of the trust.

He could claim rights of access because you would essentially be replacing one house with another."

She pauses to review a note at the bottom of the piece of paper she's holding.

"However, I think there is a workaround. If you personally finance the home either outright or make the mortgage payments out of your personal allowance, it is yours and not an asset of the trust."

"Excellent," I say with relief. The trust documents allow me a personal monthly allowance as trustee, but I rarely spend much of it. I have a sizeable amount tucked away in a savings account to which Benjamin has no access.

"If you would like to proceed, we'll get to work on breaking the prenup from the angle that you were coerced by your father."

"Yes, please, I would like to move forward with that."

"One last question," Andrea said, "why now instead of twenty years ago when your father passed away?"

I look down at my hands. "It's a story I'm sure you hear over and over. I have kept everything in a sort of stasis for the children. My sons have moved away to other states, but my daughter just graduated a few weeks ago and told me she'll be staying in Boston. Therefore, there's no need to maintain the illusion any longer."

"I understand. Do you have any questions for me?"

I think for a moment. "Do I have to wait until I sell the house before I tell Benjamin to leave?"

"It would be best. Although it was never transitioned into your names and remained as part of the trust, your father gave use of the house to the two of you as a wedding gift. Therefore, he could make a case from that angle to force you to allow him to stay. Once the house is sold and you purchase a house in your name only, he has no legal grounds to be allowed residence there."

Simon leans over and whispers to her.

"Oh yes, you could potentially pay out half the proceeds of the sale to Benjamin as a concession to avoid any appearance of personal gain, but that would be up to you." She pauses. "Is there anything else?"

I shake my head. "I think that's it for today, but if I think of something else, I'll contact you."

Ms. Hartman rises and extends her hand to me again. "Please do. It was very nice to meet you in person finally. I'll get to work on the new approach to the prenup and keep you posted."

When she extends her hand, I shake it. "I appreciate that."

"Simon will show you out."

I follow Simon back out to the lobby.

Stop bouncing! Try to act normal! I want to shout and scream and do a few hundred fist pumps in the air, but I school my face and conduct myself like a proper lady, as my mother would say.

"Have a wonderful day, Mrs. Foster," he bids me.

"You do, as well, Simon."

I am ecstatic at the outcome of the meeting. Breaking the prenuptial agreement my father had insisted upon is incredibly important. The tide is finally turning in your favor, old girl. You are about to have a whole new life and it's about damn time! I feel like singing!

I turn on the radio and crank it up. The music gives me a bit of a lead foot and I arrive at the gym before the song is over. I sit in the car singing along with Mr. Bon Jovi and crew until the song is done.

Chapter 5

Ford

I step out onto the gym floor and survey the room. It's force of habit to take stock of all the goings on whenever I enter a room. Good cops get good at noticing everything. It becomes second nature because if it doesn't, the chances of being killed on the job are high.

To call this place a gym is a bit of an understatement. It's an enormous facility, flashy and trendy. It isn't normally the kind of place I would have chosen, but they have a lot of equipment in a volume and variety that couldn't be found anywhere else in town, much less this close to my house. I can lift weights, swim, sauna, have my body hair waxed, if I were so inclined, and do Yoga all in one day.

I decide on my plan of attack for the day and start toward the weight machines. I used to be a free weights kind of guy and still use them quite a bit, but at forty-eight, I need to be more cautious.

As I get older, my body is becoming more susceptible to injuries and injuries are less likely to happen with the machines when they are used properly. I can still get a good workout in, and that's all I really care about.

All right, old man, let's get this done.

As I round the corner, I see her. This woman caught my eye the first time I came to the gym and although she doesn't know it, she played a part in my decision to join. She's my age, maybe a little younger, and she is beautiful.

She has an old-school glamor vibe. She reminds me of that gal in the old movies my mom liked to watch. What was her name again? Oh, yeah, Ava Gardner, but this woman has blonde hair.

The way she moves fascinates me. She is curvy and lush. I will never understand how women who are built like teenage boys with big fake tits came into vogue. A woman that has some softness and cushion to her can't be beat in my book.

Yeah, I noticed the gold circle with the giant rock on a certain finger, but I really like just looking at her. Not in a creepy stalker way, but women like her are a rarity these days.

Mostly because of the ring, I have never spoken to her, just appreciated the view. My shift at work has recently changed, so I am seeing her more often and I certainly won't complain about that.

She is working with a personal trainer, just like most days. He starts at one end on the weight machines and moves her down the line from machine to machine and coaches her along the way. She doesn't really seem to need much coaching or for him to push her to work harder.

She appears to push herself quite a bit, but occasionally the guy will chime in. If for nothing else, it must let him feel like he is earning his keep.

I start at the end machine in the row opposite the one where she is. We creep toward each other, moving from machine to machine. I chance a glance her way from time to time but try to concentrate on my own workout.

As we get closer, I can hear her speaking low to the trainer. She has a pleasant voice, kind of in a middle alto range and slightly husky. She probably sounds great in bed.

Cut that out. This woman is married. Admiring the view is one thing, but filling your head with fantasies about her is a little too close to the creeper line.

I move over to the chest press machine, setting the weight where I want it. I turn around and slide back onto the seat. When I have my grip where I want it, I start my first set, concentrating on keeping proper form for the full range of motion. Just as I am finishing the set, the blonde's trainer moves her to the thigh machine directly across from me.

I sit there, taking my usual break between sets and watch as the trainer gets her set up. The weight level he sets her up at means she has some strong legs. I bet they'd feel good wrapped around me.

Yeah, yeah, I still remember she's married, but maybe there's nothing wrong with a little harmless fantasizing, is there? Forget what I thought a minute ago. It's not too creeperish, right?

My dick twitch in my shorts, so I'd better put the kibosh to the fantasizing. Public fantasizing could turn into an arrestable offence in a matter of moments.

It's been a while since the last time I got laid and my dick is ready to stand at attention with the slightest notion that there's the possibility of some action. The last thing I need is to get caught ogling this enigmatic woman with a tent in my shorts.

I put my hands up to do another set just as the trainer steps back from her, signaling she's ready to start lifting. She is set up to work her inner thighs. This means that the machine presses her legs wide apart, and it is up to her to fight the weight to close her legs.

I look down at those spread legs and swallow. My eyes stroke up her body to meet hers, which go wide as her cheeks pink. She smiles and looks down quickly.

"Well, this is awkward," she says.

I can't help myself. I grin. "Not at all," I reply.

My imagination goes back to smut mode as I imagine kneeling before her and covering her sex with my mouth.

"Cait, we can move you to another machine and come back to this one, if you like," the trainer says, looking between us with a frown.

Fuck off, trainer boy.

"No, no, Tony, this is fine," she looks back at me with a crooked smile and shrugs. "We're both just trying to get our workouts in."

Good, she's got a little moxie to her.

I recall the trainer's words. Her name is Cait. Cait, what? I wonder.

I set it aside as a mystery to solve at another time and go on with my workout. We start moving away from each other again, but sometimes when I steal a glance at her, I catch her glancing right back at me.

I keep her in periphery as she finishes with the trainer and heads toward the locker room. I'm tempted to manufacture another, more personal encounter, but decide against it. She's married and I don't mess with married women.

It feels good to be a little flirty. It has been a while since have just flirted with someone. My last serious relationship was several years ago.

Since then, it has mostly been a string of one-night stands and most of those don't take much effort. I can go into just about any cop bar in the city and find a handful of badge bunnies that love to jump into bed with anyone with a shield.

The shine wore off that situation pretty quickly. If they will jump into bed with me, they will jump into bed with just about anyone else. I am too old for that shit and only indulge when I have a powerful need to get some release.

Once I finish up my workout, I go to the men's locker room. I check my watch, happy to see I have a few extra minutes to get some time in the steam room. When I emerge from the small room with a puff of mist, I'm glad I took the time to do it. I am feeling totally relaxed and ready to face the day.

I check my watch again and pick up my pace. I'd better get a move on if I'm going to get to the office on time. I'm surprised my phone hasn't gone off yet today. It's rare that I actually make it into the office first.

As I pass through the lobby toward the exit, I see the blonde, Cait, at the reception desk. I start to move closer when my phone buzzes. I pull it out and check the text.

It's the office, of course. Instead of going in, I need to go to a crime scene. I text back an affirmative as I accidentally, on purpose, eavesdrop on Cait's conversation.

"Yes, Reba, I'm sure I want to cancel at the end of the month. That's when Tony will be leaving and without him here, I'm afraid I just won't be motivated to come as often."

"Mrs. Foster, we have other trainers who would be happy to work with you."

"Yes, I know you have other trainers, and I have worked with all of them. None of the others are a good fit for me."

"Well, you have until the end of the month. We're looking for a new trainer to take Tony's spot, so maybe the new person will work."

"Perhaps, but unless I tell you otherwise, please mark my account for non-renewal as of the end of the month."

"Yes, Mrs. Foster."

"Thank you, Reba. Have a good day."

"You, too, Mrs. Foster."

I make a mental note of the name, Cait Foster. I slip my phone into my pocket and start for the door, almost plowing into Mrs. Cait Foster, the object of my imaginings.

"Oh, I'm so sorry," she says, looking up and recognizing me, her cheeks pink again.

"It's okay," I sweep out an arm, "please, go ahead."

"Thank you, Mr. uh…"

"Pickering, Ford Pickering."

She nods. "Thank you, uh, Ford."

I grin at her as she starts toward the door again. "And you are?"

She pivots back to me, her hand fluttering to her throat. "Oh, my, where are my manners? I'm Caitlyn, Caitlyn Foster, but please call me Cait," she says. She holds out her hand and I shake it.

Her hand is small in mine, fine-boned. She has a good grip, though, not hard, but firm enough to let you know she's there.

"Nice to meet you, Cait." My phone buzzes again. I pull it out, causing my jacket to shift. Her cornflower blue eyes drift to the gun and badge on my belt.

"Are you a police officer?" she asks.

"Yes, a detective, and that is work telling me to step on it to get to a crime scene."

"Please, don't let me hold you up."

I smile at her again. "Again, it was nice to meet you, Cait. Maybe we'll work out together again sometime."

Her cheeks are pink again, and that birdlike hand nervously flutters toward her throat again. "Perhaps," she says with a twinkle in her eye.

God, she's adorable.

I tip an imaginary hat to her and head out the door to see what kind of fresh evil one human being has done to another.

Chapter 6

Caitlyn

After a breakfast of toast and tea, I sit in my office. Ben did not come home last night, which is fine by me. He only rarely stays in this house, choosing to spend most of his time elsewhere. I am relieved because I don't think I could have stood looking at his face for another day.

He only comes around when it is getting close to the end of the month, as if letting me see his face will remind me to pay out his allowance. He's going to have a rude awakening at the end of this month. The gravy train has officially hit the end of the line.

My office is my favorite space in the house, and I often retreat to this room and just stare at the walls while I think about my life. This morning, my thoughts linger on the handsome stranger I met at the gym. When I saw Ford Pickering, my stomach had done a little flip-flop. Tall, and his dark hair is just starting to gray at the temples. His eyes, though, they are a brown so rich that I've never seen the like.

He isn't traditionally handsome, but there is something about him. Something a little dangerous. Then he smiled and his face was completely transformed. That smile had made me gasp and my stomach had gone all aflutter.

I shiver at the memory, needing to do something and get out of my head before I go upstairs and make use of my battery operated boyfriend. With a notepad in hand, I start making a list of things I need to take care of.

A visit to my middle child, Tommy, is long overdue. That's my highest priority. Although we talk every week and email often, it has been months since I have seen his face in person and wrapped my arms around him and his partner, Kris.

My next priority is to work on getting rid of this house and finding a new one. That includes evaluating the contents here and seeing what I want to take with me, what I want to sell, and what I want to donate.

I put down my pen and pull out the silver letter opener shaped like a sword that was a gift from my best friend. I want to see what arrived in the mail the previous day. The bundle is large, so I sort it, putting the catalogs and magazines into one pile and all the letter sized envelopes into another.

From between two magazines, an odd sized envelope slips out. It is a dark purple color, and my address is embossed in gold script. I turn it over to find the flap sealed with a stylized S and B. Inside is a card with a simple message.

You are invited to join La Société Belladone.

A website address is printed at the bottom of the card in a small font along with an invitation code. The Belladonna Society... is it supposed to mean the society of beautiful women or the society of women who might poison your ass? Maybe both, I chuckle to myself.

I start my laptop and key in the web address. The About Us page makes me think of an old gentlemen's social club my father used to belong to. It is an invitation only club with a fitness center, private dining, philanthropic drives, other regular activities, and networking opportunities.

The address shows that it is located in midtown. I need a new fitness facility. This place wouldn't be as convenient as my current location, but the added amenities would make it worthwhile.

Also, I'm on the verge of transforming from the duty driven Cait who has spent the last twenty-five years caring for family and home into...well, I'm not sure who the new Cait will be. She will be different, for sure. Plus, she'll be moving soon and could relocate somewhere more convenient to the location.

I click on the tab to join and plug in the invitation code I have been provided. *Welcome, Caitlyn Foster,* is the message that appears with a line showing an annual membership fee of $10,000. I gasp and sit back in my chair. Ten. Thousand. Dollars?

I stop. It isn't like I can't afford it and wasn't I pondering on making changes in my life just a few minutes ago?

Yes, you were.

I can do with some new connections, and I am always willing to take part in philanthropic efforts. Before I can talk myself out of it, I input my personal credit card information and click submit. I feel excited to be facing a new adventure, if even a small, albeit expensive one.

I look at the clock and realize that I had better get moving. There's just time to shower and dress for the regular weekly lunch with Monica and some of our friends.

I arrive at the restaurant with a few minutes to spare and find the group sitting at our usual table. I breeze in and take my usual chair. Hell, even my lunch bunch is stuck in a rut.

"Hello everyone! Sorry I'm late. I got caught up with things at home and lost track of time." I am assured by everyone that I wasn't late, as I expect them to do. That's what we always do when someone isn't fifteen minutes early.

I smile and look around at their faces. "So what did I miss?"

"Nothing at all," says Monica as she reaches over to pat my hand. "We only just got seated ourselves and ordered drinks. I asked for your usual water with lemon."

When the server comes with our drinks, I deviate from the *usual* and request a Chardonnay. Monica looks at me with raised eyebrows.

"I have nothing else going on today and one glass of wine is not enough to make me inebriated. It's time to start mixing things up," I say.

Monica gives me a sly smile and clinks her water glass with mine. "It's about time, sister."

We settle into the usual gossip, and everyone orders their usual lunch selections except me. I decide that after the light breakfast, I am not in the mood for yet another grilled chicken salad. Instead, I order the salmon special that comes with the usually off limits roasted baby potatoes swimming in butter.

"Sheryl," I start, trying to maintain an air of nonchalance, "how is the real estate market right now?"

"It's not bad," she reports. "It's pretty well balanced between buyers and product right now, but there aren't as many higher end homes available, so they're doing a bit better. Why do you ask? Do you know someone who's in the market?"

"Yes. I am," I drop the bombshell directly into the middle of the table, leaving my friends stunned.

Sheryl sputters. "You? In selling or buying?"

"Both," I tell her. "With the kids gone, it's just too much house. Ben Jr. is in Los Angeles and Tommy's in Denver. Maggie told me at her graduation that she's been offered a permanent position with the firm in Boston she interned with, so she will be staying in New England. I like Gaillardia. There are a couple of smaller homes in the neighborhood that might be okay, but I'm open to other locations."

"I'd be happy to help," Sheryl says, putting her hand over mine. "Let's get together later this week and we'll talk things over."

"Thank you, Sheryl, I appreciate it. I'll call you and we'll set up an appointment."

We eat for a while longer. I wasn't going to say anything, but feel compelled to ask when there is a lull in conversation, "Have any of you ever heard of La Société Belladone?"

Sheryl, sitting directly across from me, rounds her eyes, leaning forward, and says in a whisper, "The Belladonna Society?"

"Yes," I affirm. "Why are you whispering?"

"It is the most exclusive women's club in the US. Not just the City, the U fricken S. I heard Sloan Stimson got invited last year, and she went from being a mid-level manager at Johnson and Bailey to being CEO at Paige and Loftus and it was all because of her connections at the Society," Sheryl says, still whispering.

"Why do you ask?" queries Francine.

"I received an invitation to join in the mail," I say.

Monica squeals and does a little hop in her seat. "Did you join?"

"I'm thinking about it," I say.

"I wonder why they invited you," Francine ponders.

Monica turns fiery eyes on her, but I jump in before she has a chance to say anything. "Why do you say that, Francine?"

Francine shrugs. "Well, you have your family's money, but it's not like you do anything."

"Apparently, despite being a friend, you've forgotten about my involvement with several charities over the years. I've also been a board member of the Women's Coalition for the past ten years."

Maybe it's Francine's comment. Or maybe it's because of what they said about the organization. Whatever it is, I feel the need to keep it secret that I have already paid the membership fee.

"Thinking about it?" asks Sheryl. "What on earth is there to think about?"

"I probably will," I answer, "but it's not cheap."

"I imagine not," says Francine, looking at me speculatively.

"How much?" asks Monica. "No, don't tell us. I don't want to know because it's probably way more than I could ever dream of forking over for a club membership."

I smile and sip my wine. Why on earth would such an exclusive and prominent women's club be in Oklahoma City, of all places? Wouldn't it be more at home in a city like New York or Los Angeles?

We finish lunch by our usual time so that Monica and Sheryl can get back to work. Francine is a stay-at-home-mom, or so she says. She doesn't work, but rarely stays at home with the children, either. There are a couple of nannies for that.

When I arrive home, I open my email and find a welcome message from the Society. Included is a link to schedule an orientation session where I will receive a tour of the club, have dinner, and receive my pass key and other associated information. I check my calendar and decide to go on Thursday evening.

Chapter 7

Ford

Y ou would think that all the paperwork I've done first on a typewriter and now on a computer would have developed better typing skills in me. Unfortunately, I'm still a hunt and peck kind of guy.

A four-foot tall stack of papers is dropped on my desk. Okay, so maybe it's only one foot tall, but it's still a lot. "What's this?" I ask my partner.

"Finally got phone records for the last Mannekiller victim. Aaaand, the connections through one of the dating sites she was on, so now we get to go through it all."

I sigh. This is the meat of detective work. It takes time and an enormous amount of diligence to go through endless amounts of minutiae. Then completing a mountain of paperwork.

"Do you want the phone records or the dating profiles?" I ask.

"Phone records. I glanced at a few of those dating profiles and thought I was gonna lose my lunch."

I start putting the profile names and other basic information into a spreadsheet one of our data people developed for us.

This will allow us to compare information from the first three victims.

The latest one officially made our guy a serial killer. Three is the magic number, and she was victim number three. I just hope we find something to catch him before there's a number four.

Jim peels off the top third of the stack and goes to his desk. We work in silence in the ever present buzz of the station, our slow pecking on the keyboards providing a rhythm to the passing of time.

Just as we're getting into a groove, there comes the other consistent part of policing, the interruption. My phone buzzes and I answer. "Pickering."

I make notes as I listen to the dispatcher, then mark my place in the stack and lock it into a drawer. "Got a call, Jim."

He sighs, whether with relief or frustration, I can't be sure. "Whadda we got?" he asks as he levers himself out of his desk chair.

"Don't know yet. We're going to have to sort out the mess. Two dead, for sure."

"All right. You driving, or me?"

I pull out my keys in answer. Jim drives like an eighty-year-old lady, and takes forever to get anywhere. Sometimes I think he does it on purpose, so he won't have to drive. We're needed on the scene before next week, so I don't make a fuss.

We're both nearing retirement age and while I can't see myself leaving the force anytime soon, Jim seems determined to grind to a slow halt, doing as little as possible to get him to the finish line. He talks about moving to the Florida Keys and buying a boat, but I wonder where he's going to find the energy.

As I drive, I think about Cait, wondering if I'll see her tomorrow. The woman is married; I remind myself. However, she was being a little flirty with me and if my read on her is right, and it usually is, she's not the type to cheat wantonly.

That only makes my curiosity about her stronger. Maybe she's widowed and just hasn't been able to bring herself to take off the ring. I want to find out her story, but I've been so busy with my caseload that I haven't had a chance to look her up.

"What do you think about our serial? Think we're close to catching him?" Jim asks.

"Nope. I don't think we'll find him on a dating site, and I don't think we'll find him with phone records. I'd like nothing better than to put him away, but I think we're barking up the wrong tree."

"What do you think we should be doing?"

"Exactly what we are doing. Although I don't think it will yield any results, we still have to be thorough. I think he's finding them some other way, though. He's too smart to use a dating site."

"A truly random serial is almost impossible to catch until he fucks up," Jim observes.

I stare out the windshield for a while, thinking. There's only one thing all the women have in common. They don't use the same dating sites, although all of them use at least one. There's no common church, job, gym, or social groups.

"All the women told family or friends about strange occurrences in their homes, but no one took them seriously, probably because the victim played it off. I think he enjoys playing with them before he kills them, going into their homes and messing with stuff. He does just enough so they notice, but not enough to override a woman's inclination to second-guess herself."

We pull up to the address we were given by dispatch. Jim and I get out and go to the cluster of officers around a truck that's stuck in the ditch.

"What do we have, guys?"

Woody Hurt, a jovial guy with a round red face, speaks first. "Logan County found a kid walking north down the road after someone called them because the kid had red streaks all over his clothes. About the same time, we get a call from Mr. Bellew here about the truck stuck in the ditch in front of his house."

Woody leads me around to the back of the truck where the tailgate is open and there are red marks in the bed that appear to be a blood trail where a body was dragged out.

"Do we have the kid?"

"Yeah," Woody says. "Logan County brought him back and we've verified this is the kid's dad's truck. Oh, and he looks like he's about fourteen, but we verified his ID and he's not a minor. Just turned nineteen a month ago. Units were sent to the family home and there's blood evidence there, too. Crime scene techs are working the location."

"Good. Has the kid said anything?"

"Nah. We haven't tried talking to him. Figured we'd wait for you guys."

"Thanks, Woody."

"Sure thing."

Jim, who's been listening to our exchange, raises an eyebrow at me in question. I sigh. Woody leans in, "No offense, Ford, but Jim better take a shot at him. Kid's got a few neo-nazi tattoos."

"Got it. Thanks again Woody."

So the kid will respond better to the white cop than he would to the black one. All in a day's work, but it still chaps my hide. Jim shakes his head then goes and sits in the front seat of the patrol car the kid's in.

Hours later, the picture of the kid's deeds comes together. He confessed to killing his step-mother, but claimed it was an accident. Shooting someone once could conceivably be an accident.

However, when you have a two shot gun, and the victim has three bullet wounds, that means the doer had to stop and reload to shoot the third time. Kind of impossible to cry accident when that happens.

The kid also tried to cover up the crime. He painted over the blood spatter on the wall, not realizing that without some kind of primer, the blood would show through. There was paint everywhere.

After giving up on painting, the kid loaded the body into the truck and thought he'd find a place to bury it in some woods somewhere. He found a location, but was too lazy to dig a hole, so he left the body in some tall grass.

The clincher was when he led Jim right to the body. Still, the kid claimed it was an accident. Despite the evidence saying otherwise, his father ran out and hired a high-powered attorney to defend the kid. I doubt it will help him, though.

Days like today make me think twice about retiring. Sometimes the horrible things people do to each other wears me plumb out. For now, I'll get some dinner and go home.

Tomorrow's another day.

Chapter 8

Caitlyn

I wake feeling languid. I think about skipping this morning's workout. Then I remind myself that it will be one of the last times I will have Tony as my trainer and roll out of bed. I have enjoyed Tony. He is just the right blend of pushy, supportive, and helpful.

While I am dressing, I think about Detective Pickering. Inspired by the thought of possibly seeing him again, I opt for something more colorful than my usual all black ensemble.

I study myself for a moment. The color looks good on me. I think about other ways I've gotten stuck in a rut, thinking of my hair and the clothes I wear on a daily basis.

Perhaps it was for the kids in an attempt to exude motherliness in every way, but I have gotten stuck in matron mode, and I don't want to be stuck there anymore. I check myself in the mirror one last time. When the diamond on my wedding set catches the light, sending prismatic rainbows about me, I pause.

I work it off my finger and drop it into the small porcelain dish on my dresser. One final once over and, with a bounce in my step, I head out to the gym.

"What's wrong with you today, Cait? You seem distracted," Tony observes.

"I'm sorry Tony. I've just got a lot on my mind today."

The truth is that I only have one thing on my mind, or really, one person. I had hoped to see Detective Pickering again, but so far, he has been a no show.

I know I am being silly. A grown woman shouldn't be all gaga about some man, even if he is the first one to pay any attention to me in the past twenty-plus years. It was fun to flirt, and I was hoping to do some more of it today. Sadly, it is apparently not to be. I put him out of my mind and try to focus on the proper form for my reps.

"That's better," says Tony, nodding.

By narrowing my mindset, I focus on being present with every push, pull, lift, and stretch. My muscles begin the familiar burn as I test their limits. I enjoy this feeling because it makes me feel strong every time.

If only I could be strong in other ways. Emotionally, I feel beaten down because of all the years with Ben. I have put up with so much crap from him. Thankfully, there might be a way to end it all by breaking the prenuptial agreement, but I won't be too fervent in my hope. If I do, and Andrea's plan doesn't work out, it will be all the more devastating.

Freedom is what I want. I could probably do whatever I want with whomever I want, just as Ben has done. There is nothing regarding infidelity mentioned in the prenuptial document at all.

However, I am not sure I can so simply justify that kind of eye for an eye approach to wantonly jumping in bed with whomever presents themselves. Part of me likes that my history held up next to his will look lily white. It is petty, but I feel more than a little self-righteous about it.

I haven't had sex with anyone but my vibrator in a tremendously long time, but if I meet someone interesting who could be understanding of my situation...

"Good morning, Cait."

My eyes fly open to see the very man I had been thinking of earlier, Ford Pickering. He is smiling that crooked smile at me as if he has read my thoughts. My cheeks go warm.

Damn it, you're not some starry-eyed waif. Pull yourself together!

I take a breath and smile back at him. "Good morning, Ford. How are you today?"

"I'm just peachy," he replies, "and the day just keeps getting better."

I watch him walk to the machine on the end, then bend over and adjust the weight. He has a very nice backside.

"Cait," Tony says, flatly, "are you ready to get back to work?"

"Yes, sorry," I apologize and focus on the training. As we go through the machines, I occasionally slide my eyes to glance at Ford and sometimes find him looking back, an amused smirk on his face. He seems like he would be fun to play with.

When I finish the circuit on the machines, I decide to do some laps in the pool, not ready to leave. We had been almost finished with the weights and Ford was just starting, so he would be awhile.

I feel silly, chastising myself for waiting around, trying to orchestrate another chance meeting, as if that ever works out the way it is supposed to. Common sense gets the better of me after only a few laps. I step out of the pool and head to the showers.

I take my time in the shower. My skin feels sensitized. If Ford can influence my body this much with a simple greeting and smile, I wonder what would happen if he actually laid hands on me; I might spontaneously combust. My hand slips between my legs, not surprised to feel the slick, viscous evidence of my arousal.

I am so aroused that when I slip a finger between my cleft and stroke it across my clitoris, my whole body shivers. My hand presses against the shower wall to steady myself. I can't believe that I am considering masturbating right here, right now, in this semi-public environment.

Benjamin is the only man I've ever had sex with and that was behind the closed door of our bedroom. The thought of Ford Pickering is leading me into temptation, though. Joining the first finger with a second, I begin to rub circles with the flats of my fingers pressed against my clitoris.

I wonder if Ford's fingers are rough or soft. Then the crazy thought pops into my head of what it would feel like to have his stubbled cheeks grazing against my inner thighs...

I have to bite my lower lip to keep from crying out when the orgasm surges through my body with surprising force. It takes me a moment before I trust my balance enough to take my hand off the wall. The last time I masturbated was months ago, so I suppose I had been due for an intense one.

Honestly, I am surprised that my clit hasn't shriveled up from disuse.

Once I dry off and dress, I only put on a minimal amount of makeup, figuring it will only be by the most extreme luck that my path crosses with the handsome detective again today. I am more disappointed by that than I should be since I have only said hello to the man twice. After one last look in the mirror, I make sure I've gathered all my things and head for the door.

My cell phone buzzes in my bag. I juggle the bag, trying to keep a grip on it and unzip it at the same time. My inattention causes me to walk right into a wall. A wall with hands. Hands that grip my upper arms in a firm but gentle grasp.

"Whoa there, Cait," a familiar baritone voice says.

I look up to meet exploring dark brown eyes that are dancing with humor. "Ford! Oh, I'm so sorry! It seems I'm intent on running over you." My neck flushes with the heat of embarrassment.

Why can't I stop blushing around this man?

"You okay?" he asks.

I let out a breathy laugh. "Yes, I was just trying to dig my phone out of my bag and wasn't paying attention," I reply. "I'm not normally so clumsy."

The humor in his eyes warms. I wonder what he is thinking when I realize he is still holding onto my arms, his thumbs stroking across my biceps.

"I missed working out with you today," he says.

"You were later than usual," I reply, telling him what he already knows.

"That I was. Work," he says by way of explanation. "I hated to miss it since you'll be leaving soon."

My hand flutters to my throat. It is a nervous habit that I picked up from my mother. "Yes. My trainer is leaving and I'm afraid I won't be motivated to come if he's not here."

"Maybe you just need a workout partner instead of a trainer."

I raise my eyebrows. "Is that an offer, Detective?" I am shocked at my brazenness, but I do my best not to show it. Am I really flirting with him?

"It could be, Cait." His smile is warm when he says it. He lets go of my arms, leaving the warmth of his touch behind. "I tell you what, here's my card. If you want to get together for a workout or even just a coffee, give me a call."

I take the card he pulled from an inside pocket of his jacket. The same jacket that is buzzing. He pulls out his phone and looks at the screen with a scowl. "Sorry, work again. Can I walk you out?"

"Certainly," I reply, moving toward the door he indicates with his outstretched hand. His other hand goes to my elbow.

We make it through the door, and he returns his hand to my elbow. "My car is just over there," I say, waving my hand.

I watch him with my peripheral vision. He is looking everywhere. Noticing everything. I start chattering, my nervous brain coming up with such scintillating topics as the weather and how full the parking lot is.

I unlock my car and turn to face him. "Thank you, Ford."

"You're welcome. Don't forget to check your phone to see who called. Tell them I said thank you," he says with a wink.

I smile at him. "I'll do that." I don't know what possesses me, but I put my palm flat on his chest and say, "Be safe at work, Ford."

"Will do. Good to see you again, Cait."

"Good to be seen," I retort as I get into my car.

His lips spread into a lopsided grin as he tips his non-existent hat at me before he turns to walk away. I fan myself with the card he's given me as I watch him walk toward a plain sedan parked a few spaces away. Once he has driven away, I remember my phone and pull it out.

I am excited when I see who it is. I return the call. "Hi Betsey! Tell me you have an opening."

Chapter 9

Caitlyn

I open the door to Sheryl and a photographer. She sent me a contract to list the house yesterday, and we have been able to do everything electronically except the photographs. I told her to list it for however much she felt was best. I am more concerned about selling quickly than I am about making a few extra dollars.

"Oh. My. Gaaawd!" she exclaims. "I love your hair!"

"Thank you!" I reply, as I greet her with a hug. "I decided it was time for a change."

When I left Ford yesterday, the voicemail from the call I had missed when I walked into him was from my hairdresser who was happy to squeeze me in. She has been trying to get me to update my style for years. The new style plays up the natural wave in my hair and is much easier to maintain than the boring blown-out bob.

After I left the salon, I went shopping and spent more money on myself than I have in years. I got some new clothes and even some new, sexier underwear. The woman at the makeup counter was beaming when she ran my card because I had told her to wrap up everything she recommended.

Riding the roll of change, when I arrived home, I started pulling clothes out of the closet and tossing them onto the bed. Anything what was beige or neutral was scrutinized and most of it was thrown out. Well, not exactly thrown out, but out of my closet.

The mountain of clothes was bagged up and put into the back of my car along with the other items I'd been setting aside to donate. The entire load was taken to a local charity I like to support.

Sheryl and I speak in low voices as we follow the photographer around and watch her work. "Would you be willing to let the furnishings and art go with the home?" she asks me.

"Yes, except for a few of the pieces of art, I would."

"Great. A friend of mine has a buyer on the line that's looking to have a home here in the metro area and they're looking for something fully furnished and appropriate for a family. She won't tell me for sure, but I think it's a potential new Thunder player," Sheryl tells me.

"If they're the least bit interested, make it happen. I'm willing to give them a great deal," I say.

"Have you thought about where you might like to move?" she queries.

"Like I said at lunch, I like this neighborhood," I tell her again. "However, I've been thinking about it, and I think maybe I could do with a change. There are a few locations I'd consider, like Nichols Hills or Heritage Hills. I'd prefer a gated community since I'll be living alone, but I could be persuaded otherwise for the right property."

"Living alone? What about Ben?" she asks, clearly confused.

Damn. I hadn't meant to say that. Being with a friend lulled me into dropping my guard and loosening my lips. I sigh. "His latest is pregnant, and he's spending most of his time with her. This is not for general consumption, but the new property will be purchased by me and will be in my name only. I won't be using funds from the trust."

"That bastard," she swears. "Good for you, honey."

After that, I'm more careful with my words. I consider Sheryl to be trustworthy, but it is just common sense that if you don't want something to get around, the best thing to do is not to talk about it at all.

I am too comfortable with my friends, and I use that term loosely. Monica is the only one of my lunch bunch I'd consider a genuine friend. Sheryl is more like a close acquaintance and Francine, well, she may stop coming after our last get together, but I wouldn't mind that after her comments.

I absolutely do not want any word of me working with the new attorney to leak. My goal is for Ben to remain in the dark as long as possible. If I can manage a quick sale on the house and be moved into a new location before he finds out, all the better.

It takes the photographer a while to finish. The house is enormous, so it's not surprising. Sheryl and I discuss timing to put a sign in the yard and when it should go live online.

We come to an agreement that she's not exactly happy about, but I can convince her I have my reasons for not acting aggressively too quickly. I cross my fingers that her lead on a quick sale will come through and enable me to avoid the whole mess of showings and such. She suggests I pull any items I want to keep and start boxing them up to put into storage so that, should things move quickly, I can be as prepared as possible to vacate right away.

I have a couple of hours before I need to get ready for the Belladonna Society orientation that evening, so I walk through the house with a pad of paper making notes of items I want to keep. The kids have already cleared out their rooms mostly, but I will still need to go through them. I collected mementos through the years and have a box for each child, but I should double-check to ensure that nothing has been overlooked. I make a note of that, as well.

I linger in each of the children's rooms. All three of them are grown up, full-fledged adults but they will always be my babies. Even Ben Jr. who is so much like his father it makes my heart hurt, is still my first love in my mind's eye.

My mother's love was there, but it was always overshadowed by her devotion to my father. I had never felt love, I mean truly felt it to the core of my being, until I'd held my firstborn in my arms for the first time.

Although I love Ben Jr., our relationship is tenuous, at best. He treats people like pawns on the game board of his life. He uses them for what he can get from them, and the only thing he wants from me is his inheritance.

I am close with my younger two, and miss them terribly even though I just saw Maggie a few weeks ago.

My list is shorter than I'd thought it would be when I finish, but that's fine. The less I need to get moved out, the faster I can get it taken care of. I can't sell this house fast enough. I am sick of it, sick of it all. I am so ready for change and not just in my living accommodations.

In my office, I leave the notepad and pen on the desk where I see Ford's business card sitting on the blotter where I'd left it. I stretch out a finger to touch the heavy paper. Ford Pickering is a potentially positive change for the better.

Maybe he will just be a harmless flirtation. However, if I am honest with myself, I am interested in doing more than flirting, a whole lot more. If that happens, we'll definitely have to have a conversation about my marital situation, which may put him off, shutting things down before they even get started. I will just have to cross that bridge when and if I come to it.

With a glance at my watch, I see I need to get ready for the orientation session, so I hurry upstairs to shower and dress, eager to wear one of my new outfits.

Chapter 10

Ford

I arrive at the crime scene, pulling latex gloves and covers for my shoes out of the pack on the passenger seat. The apartment complex is fairly new, but a quick look tells me there aren't any surveillance cameras in use widely on the property. The victim's apartment is ideally situated to allow for ingress and egress with the least possibility of being spotted.

She had probably liked it because being on the end with no other buildings directly on her side made for a quieter existence. Complexes like this, with their highly transient clientele, are shit for building a community where the neighbors watch out for each other. Most of the time, they never get to know their neighbor's names before they're replaced by new neighbors.

After making a circuit of the building, I climb the stairs to the third floor. Even with the police presence and flashing lights, I go all but unnoticed. "What do we have, Pete?" I asked the officer guarding the entrance to the apartment.

"Another weird one, Detective," Pete replies.

When I enter the apartment, I see the latest victim of the serial killer we've been chasing. Three is the magic number that turns a regular killer into a serial. This is the fourth in a series of murders that spans across the last six months with approximately two months between each murder.

The rumor mill around the precinct is calling this guy the Mannekiller because of the way he leaves his victims posed like mannequins. Personally, I don't think they deserve any other name besides guilty piece of shit, and I hate the way some people need to make pseudo-celebrities out of some criminals.

I make a wide circuit around the body, staying out of the way of the crime scene techs who are still documenting everything in its current state. They're putting down markers, so that means they've been here long enough to document the scene with the initial photographs.

They start by photographing the room from every angle in concentric circles. Once that is complete, they move in and start identifying evidence. Markers are placed and they'll photographically document everything again in wide-view and close-up.

I stop to watch the techs work while talking to one of the first officers on the scene.

"We got a call from her sister, who came over to do a wellness check. The victim's name is Anna Thompson. She didn't show up at work and her family hasn't been able to get in touch with her all day. Her sister has a key to the place and came over after work to check the apartment. She came inside and when it was clear that the victim was deceased, she went back to the entry and called 911," the officer reports.

"Is that the sister in the living room?" I ask.

"Yes."

"Thanks," I tell him.

I observe the victim where she sits. She was tied to a barstool so that she would remain in an upright position even after rigor had come and gone. Her arm is propped onto the counter with her fingers touching a glass.

The glass contains liquid which, I am sure, will prove to be her drink of choice. She is dressed as if she is out on a date. If I close my eyes, I can picture her sitting just that way in a bar, waiting for a date to arrive.

I think that is a plausible angle. All three of the victims have been dressed to catch a man's attention and posed like this, as if they were waiting at a bar for a date, each with their preferred drink.

I am sure this one will prove to have been sexually assaulted as well. I can hope, but I am fairly sure there will be no trace evidence left behind. All the evidence has suggested that the sex was all post-mortem, so he could take his time cleaning up, making sure he didn't miss a thing.

My stomach turns just thinking of it. How does someone get off on fucking a corpse? There's no movement, no life, only cold flesh. Perhaps to him, it's the ultimate control or insult. I'm no head shrinker, so I don't know.

The killer is meticulous. He is still systematic in his methodology, which means he is unlikely to make a mistake. Mistakes don't usually happen until a serial is escalating, needing to kill more often and take more chances to keep the thrill alive. That could take months, or even years, to occur.

Once I've taken everything in visually, it is a waiting game to see what forensics comes up with. I make my way to the living room to question the sister. The woman is sitting with an officer, but they're not speaking.

She looks up at me with a tear-streaked face as I quietly introduce myself. I take the seat across from her and start asking questions, doing my best to be conciliatory and comforting. My goal is to get to know the victim from her sister's viewpoint and about those closest to her.

When I finish, my suspicions are confirmed. The information gathered from the sister's description of this latest victim is very similar to the other three victims.

They have all been between twenty-five and thirty-five. Moderately successful in their professional lives, but unsuccessful when it came to love. They are all members of online dating sites, but their families are unsure of which one or if there were multiple.

The sister also says the victim had mentioned strange things happening in her apartment. Items not being where she remembered leaving them. A towel on the floor in the bathroom that she was sure was hanging when she left.

I'm really starting to hate this fucker.

Her computer and phone are taken from the scene. It takes weeks or sometimes even months to get their cell phone records from their providers. Things don't turn on a dime like they do on television. If I had known how much frustrating waiting and paperwork were involved in the reality of detective work, I might have remained a patrol officer.

It's late, and I think about going home, but if I do that, I'll need to go in early to type up the reports related to the night's work. That would mean I wouldn't be able to go to the gym. With my opportunities to see the adorable Cait Foster in her curve hugging workout clothes running out at the end of the month, I turn toward the station.

I sit down at my desk and pull out my notebook. When I flip it open, I see the page where I had noted a tag number. I'll pull it up before I leave, but it's best to get the reports out of the way first.

Two hours later, my reports are submitted, and I shut down my computer. I pinch the bridge of my nose as I stand, a headache creeping in from staring at the screen for too long. Gathering up my things, I head for the door.

Flipping my notebook closed, I catch sight of the page with the tag number again. Rather than restart my antique computer, which would take several minutes, I stop at the front desk.

"Hey Betty, will you do a favor for me and run this tag? I meant to do it before I logged out and forgot."

"Sure," Betty replies. "Got a suspect?"

"I don't think so. Just someone I want to follow up with."

When the information comes up, she looks at me skeptically. "Follow up with, huh?" She clicks some keys on her keyboard and I hear her printer come to life. When the document is finished, she hands it across the counter to me. "She's pretty."

"Thanks Betty," I say with a grin. "Have a good night!"

I slide into the driver's seat of the department issued sedan and turn on the dome light. When I read the report, it is confirmed, Caitlyn Foster is officially out of my league.

Not only out of my league, she's out of my dimension, my entire solar system. She lives in fucking Gaillardia, one of the wealthiest neighborhoods in the entire metro area.

I'd had my suspicions. There is something about the way she dresses, speaks, and carries herself that conveys class, but she isn't flashy. The car she drives is a Mercedes, but it is very old.

I wonder if it is her money or her husband's. If she has a husband. She had been wearing a wedding ring every time I had seen her until yesterday.

Had she left it off because something had happened, or maybe because of him? Maybe she is a widow, and she decided it was time to leave it in the jewelry box.

I sigh, too damn tired to think about it. I still hope I see her in the morning at the gym.

What a sap.

Chapter 11

Caitlyn

I pull up to a building on the edge of midtown and automobile alley. It is an old building, three stories of squat red brick, lit up like Christmas. It stands out because most of the surrounding buildings are dark after the close of business hours.

I flip down the mirror on the visor to put on some lipstick before I get out, and admire my new hair style again, still amazed at the difference it makes. I feel a little nervous. This is a completely new experience for me.

For the past twenty-six years, my life has been tied up with husband, children, and home. At forty-five, I haven't accomplished anything besides taking over my family's trust, not even finishing college. I dropped out as soon as I found out I was pregnant with my first child.

Francine's words haunt me. What does someone like me have to offer an organization like this? Although the fact I've stayed with Benjamin even after he'd cheated on me repeatedly might indicate otherwise, I consider myself to be fairly intelligent.

There is the fact that I have a whole lot of money. And connections. People always want to know those who have deep pockets and there are plenty who want to know me. I have a few very close friends, but a boatload of acquaintances in all manner of walks of life. Yes, I have something to offer and I'm going to make the most of it.

I straighten my spine and get out of the car. When I push inside, there is a large foyer, two and a half stories tall, pressing into the heart of the building. Everything is cream and gold with touches of charcoal and royal purple, elegant and classy, without being over the top.

At the end of the entry is another set of double glass doors. I push through those to find a reception area that is more of the same high-end elegance. A young woman, tall and willowy, dressed in classic chic, is behind the desk and another person is standing to one side. I am pretty sure that person is also a young woman, but because of the androgenous appearance, I can't be sure.

Either way, the person is striking with short, inky hair in a style that reminds me of a pompadour over very alert, brilliant cerulean eyes. She or he, or maybe even they, is dressed in a fitted suit. "Mrs. Foster," the person says, extending their hand. "My name is Victoria, and I will be your guide this evening."

I shake the proffered hand. "Victoria, it's very nice to meet you."

"Your orientation session will be with four other new members, and we are still waiting for two to arrive. If you don't mind following me, I'll take you to the others where you can get better acquainted while you wait. Please come this way." She gestures toward a door.

We go through the door to a room that is styled much like a lounge with comfortable sofas arranged to allow easy conversation. Two women are sitting there. One is young, maybe in her late twenties, with alabaster skin and long blond hair. She has intelligent blue eyes. She looks vaguely familiar, but I cannot place her.

The other woman appears to be my age, but her dark skin is so smooth and unlined that I can't be sure. She sits with a ramrod straight spine on the sofa, her bearing self-assured and regal. Her ebon hair is smoothed and pulled into a tight bun at the base of her neck.

I cross the room to the women and introduce myself. "Hello, my name is Caitlyn Foster."

"Serena Chilton," the regal woman says with a slight nod of her head.

"Demeter Lawson," says the younger woman with a broad smile.

"I guess we're waiting for two others," I say.

I start to go on, hoping to begin a conversation since it appears that the other two were just sitting and waiting rather than talking when I entered. However, the door opens again to reveal another one of our group. The woman has long dark hair and tan skin. She smiles as she approaches us, but I can tell she's nervous.

Years of experience playing hostess kicks in. "Hello! Please join us," I tell her. "My name is Caitlyn Foster. This is Serena Chilton and Demeter Lawson." I gesture at the other women as I introduce them.

"I'm Gabriella Carmichael," the newcomer says as she takes a seat.

"Hello Gabriella." I look at the others with a smile. "I wasn't sure what to expect coming here. Everything leading up to this moment seemed so cryptic and mysterious."

That gets a chuckle out of them, and everyone relaxes a bit. I continue leading the charge. "Serena, what made you decide to join?" I ask.

"Well, I guess I was mostly hoping to get to know some new people. I am new at the university in Norman this year and hanging out after hours with the same people I spend my days with isn't always appealing. Sometimes I simply do not want to talk shop," she says.

"Oh, I went to school at OU," Demeter says. "What do you teach?"

"I teach at the College of Law," Serena answers.

"My degree is in psychology, so I doubt I know anyone in your area," Demi says. "What about you, Caitlyn? What do you do?"

"I've been a wife and mother for the past twenty-five years, for the most part, but I sit on the board of a few charities."

"Are you affiliated with the Women's Coalition?" Demeter asks with a tilt of her head.

"Yes, yes I am," I reply.

"That's why you look familiar! Several years ago, I was a TA for Dr. Ava Stephens and sat in on a few meetings for her to take notes when she couldn't attend."

"Yes! I remember that," I tell her, glad to have placed the connection with her.

"My former fiancé, Jeremiah McLean, was also quite involved with them," she says.

My heart squeezes. "I am so sorry for your loss, Demeter. Jeremiah was such a wonderful man. I was so saddened when I learned he had passed."

She smiles, but only faintly. "Please call me Demi. Thank you for the condolences. It's been six years and I still miss him every day."

"Gabriella, what do you do?" I ask, taking the spotlight off Demi rather than continuing to dredge up heavy memories.

"I have a construction design business." Gabriella answers.

The door opens again, and Victoria enters with the last member of our orientation group, a petite woman who looks a bit harried at the moment. "I apologize for being late," the newcomer says, "a surgery ran into complications. I'm Alicia Pham."

"Are you a surgeon?" Serena asks.

"I'm still in my residency, but yes," she replies.

"Ladies, if you are ready, we will get started," Victoria says.

I am very impressed with the facilities. It is much more than a place to exercise. The lobby was a bit austere, but the rest of the facilities are like the lounge where we waited. It is warm and elegant with a comfortable, homey feel.

There is an extensive library with a fireplace and plenty of welcoming chairs. The second floor has a medical spa with an expansive variety of services as well as the fitness center, which includes personal trainers available at any time the facility is open. The third floor houses an event space along with a bar and restaurant.

Victoria leads us to a table where another woman is seated. When she sees us, she rises. She is obviously wealthy, and I recognize her from society events, Elizabeth Kaizen, whose family is one of the wealthiest in the state. She holds out her hands to me. "Cait, it's so good to see you again."

I take her hands in mine and we do the socialite's air kiss. She releases me and greets my companions. She has apparently been briefed on each one of us. "My name is Elizabeth Kaizen. I have been a member here for a few years now and I am here to welcome you and answer any questions you might have," Elizabeth says.

As soon as we take our seats, very handsome, very fit servers place menus in front of us and hover until we order. The conversation flows easily, with Elizabeth being an accomplished hostess.

Several women stop by our table to say hello, some dressed professionally, some casually, and some look as if they came to have dinner before or after working out. I am honestly astounded at the wealth and power represented in the room.

Isn't this the way it used to be in those gentlemen's clubs the invitation reminded me of? Men gathered in those settings for years to make deals and set the course of history. They probably still do.

It's about time women started coming together to wield their wealth and power in the same way. Although a lot of our money came from our male forefathers, we can put it to better use. A use that is for more than just gaining more power.

When we are almost finished eating, a very petite woman with dark hair and a birdlike build stops by our table. She looks to be in her sixties or seventies, but is still hale and hardy.

"Ladies, my name is Noémie Thiry. I am so pleased to meet you. If you need anything at all, please don't hesitate to stop by my office on the first floor."

This woman is obviously in charge. She has a French accent with a voice that is melodic and sounds like sex. She is sensual without trying. I have no doubt she could have a man eating out of the palm of her hand with just a few words, despite her advanced age.

Once she has greeted each of us with a few words, she excuses herself and moves to another table, where she talks for a few moments. She makes her way through the room, greeting and chatting. Victoria is close on her heels, surveying the room as if she's some sort of secret service agent keeping an eye out for danger.

Chapter 12

Caitlyn

Alicia excuses herself first once the meal is complete, citing an early surgery. Before she can leave, I say, "We should try to meet on Thursdays for dinner to keep in touch with each other. No pressure, just a casual thing for whenever we're available."

"I'll try," she says. "It will just depend on my schedule.""I understand," I say. "It's just a thought. Like I said, no pressure. Just come if you can."

The others say much the same about availability and schedules. Alicia's departure leads Elizabeth and Serena to leave as well. Demeter follows soon after. I chat with Gabriella a bit longer before we both decide to leave. She detours to inspect the fitness center, so we say our farewells and part ways.

When I pass back through the area I have come to think of as the lounge, I notice something. Wedged into the corner of the room is a Fortune Teller machine like I'd seen once on the boardwalk of Coney Island on vacation with my parents. I detour to get a better look at it.

Across the top in two lines, the words, Oracle Orenda then Make a Wish, are emblazoned in gothic gilt letters. I look around, but I'm the only one in the room. Nostalgia rises in me.

A vacation to New York is one of the rare, truly happy memories I have from my childhood. My mother had still been alive, and it was one of the few vacations we ever took.

My father had worked the entire time, but Mother and I had taken a day to roam the boardwalk. There were shops and games and places to eat. We had lousy food and excellent ice cream, and my mother had let me get a fortune from the machine.

The message I received was something silly, but as a girl, I thought it was the most wonderful thing I had ever seen. A message from the universe just for me. I didn't understand the meaning of it then, but I was sure that eventually all the pieces of my life would come together to reveal the hidden message and I would be amazed. Of course, that never happened.

Behind the window is a painted fortune teller, a raven-haired beauty clothed in shades of lavender, soft blue and green. She resembles the older woman who stopped by our table at dinner somewhat. Perhaps she had it made that way.

The oracle's hands are hovering over ornate cards laid out in a fan. Just below the window is a button with the instructions to press the button, then make a wish to have the answer to your wish revealed. I smile, then have a crazy thought. I press the button and whisper, "I wish my husband were dead."

Perhaps that is extreme, and I should have tempered it, but it's the first thing that popped out. Before I can amend my wish to something more socially acceptable, there is a whirring and clicking of the gears inside the machine. After a few moments, a card pops from a slot in the front. I pull it out and read the inscription.

The question you ponder, the answer you'll find, when the story you've started begins to unwind.

Feeling the need to inform fate that I really don't desire a homicide, I tell the genie in the box, "I don't really want him dead, just gone. As in, away from me. Divorced."

I study the card. The story I've started... Is that the story with the attorney? The story of selling the house? My eyes widen as a thought strikes. The story with Ford?

I know the house will sell, perhaps not as quickly as I'd like, but it's just a matter of time. I hope the story with the attorney works out because that would truly be the best outcome for everyone, especially my children. A divorce, as painful as it might be for them, is still better than a death.

Believe me, I promise I don't truly wish any harm to Benjamin, no matter what flights of fantasy I might have. I just want him to go away, and without the ability to break the prenup, I have a feeling that only death will loose his hold on my life. Something has got to give in that area because I refuse to stay in the limbo I've lived in for the past quarter century.

As for Ford, it has felt wonderful to flirt. Maybe we will do more than flirt. Maybe he will be willing to overlook my entanglement with Benjamin. I doubt that will happen, but I cheer at the thought.

However, there's always the likelihood that perhaps this fortune is just as much nonsense as the one from my childhood, and it means nothing at all. I tuck the card into my pocketbook and head toward the reception area. The woman at the desk hands me a packet containing all the information I will need, including the spa menu and fitness class schedule.

I am very pleased at how the evening has gone and elated that I decided to join. It seems as if my decision to get out of my rut is allowing the Universe to bring all manner of wonderful things across my path, including potential new friends.

It is a beautiful fall evening, so I roll down the windows and turn on the radio. When one of my favorite songs comes on, I turn it up and sing along at the top of my lungs. Although the sun has set, and I won't be able to see much, instead of immediately hopping onto the highway to go home, I drive through the Heritage Hills neighborhood that is just a few blocks from the club.

The homes are mostly large and stately, and the streets are lined with towering mature trees. It is quiet except for my singing and there are people out walking their dogs or just walking for exercise, which means it is safe. I like that.

I am still feeling great when I get home and go into the house. Instead of parking in the garage, I park in the driveway. The weather is predicted to remain clear, and I'll be leaving early to go to the gym anyway, so I don't bother to drive around back.

I walk through the dark house and go to the kitchen. With a flip of the switch, I turn on the lights and place my purse with the packet on the kitchen island, intent on getting a drink of water.

The front door bursts open when Ben enters as if he was waiting for me to get home to make a big entrance. Maybe he was hiding somewhere outside the neighborhood, waiting for me to pass by. I wouldn't put it past him.

He shouts through the house. "Cait! Where are you? Did you think I wouldn't find out?"

I put the glass down on the counter. "Find out what, Benjamin?" I query, not shouting, but loud enough for him to pinpoint my location.

"You're selling the house," he says, coming into the light.

How did he find out? There is no way to know, but just as I'd thought when I was with Sheryl, unless you do something without telling another soul, there's always the potential for others to discover what you don't want them to.

"Yes, I am," I respond, because there's no sense in denying it. "I'm the only one who lives here, and now that I know Maggie will be staying in Boston to make a life there, I've decided to sell. This place is too much house for one person."

"What do you mean, you're the only one who lives here? It's my house, too," he grits out.

I know it's unladylike, but I can't help but snort. "You may spend two or three nights out of thirty in your bedroom. I hardly call that living here."

He narrows his eyes at me. "If you sell, you have to give me half. Your father gave this house to both of us."

I shake my head. "The deed for the house is in the trust's name and therefore, an asset of the trust. I've discussed it with an attorney. If I sell, the proceeds go back into the estate."

He growls, causing me to take a step back. "My allowance is late. When is that going to be deposited into my account?"

I start to feel a little afraid. Benjamin has never scared me, but I have never seen him angry like this before, either. "Our children are grown and gone and not coming back. Therefore, I feel no need to maintain the façade that this is a happy home for them. You've moved on. I'm moving on, too."

I step around the island to fill my glass with water and put a little distance between us. "Therefore, you won't be receiving an allowance any longer. I only started giving you one to help soothe your ego since I received the allowance provided by the trust. I've decided that if you want to live with your pregnant girlfriend, you can do that with your own money."

Perhaps I could have found a gentler, more circumspect way of phrasing it, but I'm tired of trying to make everything okay for Benjamin.

He sneers. "Please tell me you're going to divorce me."

"No. I'm not. But I'm not going to support you anymore, either."

He lunges for my purse. "Give me my goddamn money, you bitch!"

We both grab it at the same time and are evenly matched. He is a man and bigger than me, but he's gotten softer while I'd been working out regularly for years. He pulls hard on the bag, but I have the straps of the well-made handbag in a firm grip. With a twist and a hard turn, he tries to leverage the bag away from me. As he does, his elbow connects with my eye.

"Ouch!" I cry out and let go of the purse. It's not like there is anything in it he can use, anyway. There are only a couple of twenties that I keep in my wallet in case I need cash for something.

He pulls out my wallet and finds the forty dollars in cash there. He takes the bills, drops the purse, and points a finger at me. "You'd better make that deposit, Cait, or I'll be back tomorrow to make you!"

A voice sounds from the hall. "You were right Jerry; you'd better call the cops. He just hit her."

Apparently, Ben had been in such a state when he came through the front gate that one of the security officers had followed him to the house out of concern for my safety. I'm not sure why he didn't call me and inform me when he arrived, but when Ben left the door open, the officer had stepped inside.

Upon hearing Ben yelling, he had come close enough to see Ben and me struggling over the purse, including the elbow to the eye.

"What the hell are you doing here?" Ben bellows at the guard.

"Sir, the police are on their way," the guard informs him.

"For Christ's sake, why'd you call the cops!" Ben glares at me then snarls, "Make that deposit, Cait, or else." He strides toward the still open front door.

"Sir! Sir! You can't leave! The police will need to speak with you!" the guard calls after him, but Ben ignores the admonition and leaves, anyway. The sound of his starting car sounds down the hallway, punctuated by the screeching of his tires as he leaves the driveway.

I reach into the freezer and take out a small bag of peas that I'd been meaning to throw away. When I put the frigid package to where Ben's elbow had connected, I wince. The cold is harsh against my skin, but the blow has left a dull ache in its wake. I hope I don't have a black eye in the morning.

I ask if we can call the police officers off, but the security guard says no, the call has to be responded to. With a sigh, I start a pot of coffee for the police officers that will be coming soon. There is a precinct office near my neighborhood and response times are fast so they should be here soon.

I pull down mugs and get out sugar and cream along with some spoons, and put them on the counter. There's nothing else to offer them. Without the children at home, I rarely keep snacks in the house anymore.

The coffee has just finished brewing when the patrol car arrives. Thankfully, there are no lights or sirens involved. I would have hated to disturb my neighbors; Ben has already done enough of that with his theatrics.

Two officers, a man and a woman, come in through the door that is still standing wide open. I offer them coffee, which they accept, then we get down to business. The security guard is taken into the living room by one officer while the other stays with me.

I go through the story several times. Officer Padilla frowns at me when I say I don't want to press charges. Although I assure her repeatedly that it was an accident, she doesn't believe me.

I know that there are many battered women who make excuses for their partner, but I let her know that if he had purposefully hit me, I would be adamant about charging him. She doesn't believe me and keeps pushing, but eventually, with sighs of frustration, they leave.

I'm not sure what to do about Ben. I have never been afraid of him before, but he was so angry tonight. He was angrier than I have ever seen him before, but I will not let that sway me from the course I have set. He is cut-off financially; I am selling this house as soon as possible, and I will find a way to cut marital ties with him once and for all.

Chapter 13

Ford

When I arrive at the precinct the next morning, I am in a shitty mood. I went to the gym this morning, but the bright spot I had hoped to have in my day was a no show. I stopped Cait's trainer to ask why she wasn't there and was told that she'd called in to say that she was feeling under the weather and wouldn't be coming in.

Betty is at the desk again. "Mornin' Betty. What are you doing back here this morning?"

"Stefan's wife went into labor early this morning, so I said I'd come in to cover his shift," she replies. "Hey, you know that address that popped on the tag you had me run last night?"

"Yeah," I grunt at the additional reminder of Cait.

"Not long after you left, we got a four-fifteen call for the same address," she informs me.

Before I can think about what I'm doing, I turn on my heel and leave the building. A four-fifteen is a domestic dispute. If her husband has laid hands on her, I will throw the man's ass in jail without hesitation.

Cait's neighborhood is only a couple of minutes from my station. I pull under the portico and up to the security window.

With a flash of my badge, I give the guard on duty Cait's address as my destination.

A gangly young guy dressed in the security company's uniform squints at my identification. "We heard about what happened," he says with a frown. "I hope she's okay. Mrs. Foster is one of the few in here that isn't a snob. She actually talks to us like we're real people."

The heavy iron gate at the entrance begins to swing open. "Thanks," I tell him.

The guard's comment gives me more insight into the woman. I thought Cait would be that way, but I appreciate his confirmation. She seems to be pure class.

I make my way through the neighborhood, following the indicators on my navigation screen. The houses here are large, so there aren't a lot of them, but the streets seem to be laid out in the most convoluted manner possible. Home after home, the luxury is astounding. I doubt there is a house less than five-thousand square feet in the entire subdivision.

I pull into the driveway and eye the enormous house through the windshield. It has to be at least ten thousand square feet. The size isn't surprising based on the neighborhood, but it doesn't look like Cait at all.

It is gray stone and looks like it is trying to mimic a European castle. It even has a fucking turret. Overall, it is cold, unwelcoming, and is nothing like Cait.

I go to the door and ring the bell, turning my back to the door, surveying the manicured lawn. The back of my neck tickles and my instincts tell me she is watching me through the peephole, trying to decide if she wants to open the door. I turn to face her.

"Let me in Cait." I don't raise my voice, just make the statement and let her decide.

I can almost hear her sigh just before the deadbolt slides free, and she opens the door to me. She steps back into shadow, holding the door open. "Good morning, Ford. Won't you please come in?"

She closes the door behind me. When she turns around, I get my first good look at her, and my blood begins to boil. Cait's left eye is blackened from a blow. I can't stop myself. I reach out to her, my hands cupping her face and gently turning it to the light so I can get a better look. "What happened, Cait?"

She looks down and away from me. "It was an accident," she says.

"Bullshit."

If I had a dollar for every time some abused woman said those words to cover up for her piece of shit abuser, I'd be a wealthy man.

She sighs. "It really was an accident. I wouldn't cover for my husband. I would be the first one to call the police if he ever purposely laid a hand on me."

"Your husband," I reply woodenly. So, she is married. Actively married.

"Technically," she says, still not looking at me. "Come in and I'll tell you everything. Would you like some coffee?"

I follow her through the house. She is dressed casually in something that looks soft to the touch. I have to admit, watching her hips sway in that soft material distracted me so much that I took no notice of the house.

We enter a kitchen that would make Wolfgang Puck jealous. The coffee smells heavenly, much better than the swill I had been about to have at the office. She pulls out two mugs and sets them on the counter.

"Do you need cream or sugar?" she asks.

"Black is fine."

She fills both mugs and hands one to me. She doctors hers with both sugar and cream. "Are you hungry? I can heat up some breakfast casserole for you."

I am hungry. I had been in such a funk after not seeing her at the gym that I'd forgotten to stop and grab something. "Sure, but quit stalling. What happened last night?"

She throws a look at me, her eyes flashing. "I will. Be patient."

I like the fire I see in her. She is not some chronically battered woman who has been beaten down by abuse. I believe that this is a first occurrence, but I know that once it happens, it gets easier for the abuser to do it again and again until it becomes a pattern.

She goes to the refrigerator, pulls out a casserole dish, and scoops a generous helping of the contents onto a plate before putting it into the microwave. As she works, she begins to speak.

"In order for last night to make sense, I need to give you some background. My husband, Benjamin, is a philanderer. He's been having affairs since about six months after our wedding, which was two and a half decades ago."

She takes a breath to continue, but I dive in with my first question. I can't help it. Gathering information is second nature, and I want all the information I can get on this woman and her asshole husband. "How does someone like you end up with someone like that?"

She pulls the plate out of the microwave and places it in front of me, along with a fork and a napkin. I take a bite, starting to wolf it down, used to eating when I have a few minutes to grab something, but when the flavor bonanza hits my taste buds, I slow down, chewing more slowly and savoring the meal.

When she put it down in front of me, I thought it was just eggs and sausage. But no, there is onion, mushrooms, peppers and a variety of seasonings. She must have added some cream because the eggs are fluffy and silky. If she can cook like this, I might just have to marry her. The fact that she is already married could be problematic, though.

"My father was very religious," she answers. "I was not allowed to date or have a boyfriend at all while I was growing up. When I went to college at eighteen, I'd never been in a relationship. The only reason my father let me go to school was because it had been my mother's dying request."

She tells me how Ben had courted her and swept her off her feet before their wedding. He had been sweet and charming, doing and saying all the right things to make her swoon. Their engagement was brief before they had the fairytale wedding of her dreams. My first thought is that Ben probably sniffed out her family's bank account and targeted her.

She goes on. "Soon, I realized my fairytale was one that must have been pulled out of the back pockets of those old Brothers Grimm. I found out about the first affair at the same time I found out I was pregnant with our first child. After that, I had two more children. Soon after I found out I was pregnant with our third, my father passed away. With his passing, I did not need to keep up the pretense of fulfilling my wifely duties and quit sleeping with my husband. That was just over twenty years ago."

Christ. Twenty years ago? I wonder if she has been with anyone since. Perhaps she has taken up emulating her husband's wandering gaze. "Why didn't you divorce him?"

She sighs again. I can tell that this isn't a story she tells many people and that living it has worn her down emotionally.

"My mother's passing took a toll on my father. He sold the family business and transferred everything into a trust. It is a substantial amount of money, so he had Ben and I sign a prenuptial agreement."

She tells me about the agreement and her father's stipulation that she could not divorce her husband for any reason. If she did, she would only receive one fourth of the amount in the trust and the rest would go to him.

I am about to jump in with another question, but she holds up a hand. Anticipating my question, she says, "If I thought he'd do right by our children, I'd divorce him in a heartbeat.

However, he would squander the money and leave them nothing."

Returning to the agreement, she gives the kicker. If Ben divorces her, he gets nothing. If Cait were to die, the trust would be divided among the children, and Ben would get nothing.

"Call me petty," she says, "but I refuse to see him awarded with close to one hundred million dollars for being a lousy husband and human being."

I swallow at the amount. I also notice that she hadn't added lousy father to the list of Ben's failings. "So, what happened last night?"

She tells me about how their children are scattered around the country and none of them intend to return to Oklahoma with her daughter making that decision only recently.

"Therefore, I have decided to sell this monstrosity and yesterday, I listed it with an agent. Ben found out, and that's initially why he came over last night. He rarely comes here anymore. He won't get anything from the sale and got mad."

She turns for the pot and refills my mug. The coffee was damn good, and I gulped it down.

"I also cut off the monthly allowance that, as trustee, I'd been giving him. He grabbed my purse, I guess hoping I had more cash in it than the forty dollars he found and took. We struggled over the bag and when he tried to jerk the purse away, his elbow accidentally hit me in the eye. It was not intentional."

"Has he ever been aggressive toward you before?" I ask.

She shakes her head. "No. I have never been afraid of him. Last night was the first time. Although this was an accident," she waves a hand at her face, "if the guard hadn't followed him to the house and witnessed what happened, I don't know that he would have stopped. Legally, because he is still listed as a resident of this house, they can't prevent him from entering the grounds."

"Does he still have keys to the house?"

"Yes. I was about to call a locksmith when you knocked."

"Call them now," I order. If her husband raises a stink, she'll have to give him new keys. Legally, unless she has some sort of protective order, she can't bar him from entering.

She rolls her eyes at me and then winces with pain. I am glad to see she still has some fight in her. She turns and walks down the hall.

I wipe my mouth and put my empty plate into the sink, then follow her. Curiosity drives me to see more of the house, particularly since I was so oblivious on the way in. I feel validated by my observation that the house didn't seem to fit Cait. Apparently, she hates it.

We walk into a room that makes my jaw drop. It is obviously an office with a very sturdy-looking desk in the center, but one entire wall is adorned with a variety of weapons and representations of weapons.

What the fuck?

For a moment, I think I'm completely wrong about this woman and she's really some kind of psychopath.

"What's this?" I ask, waving a hand at the wall.

She smiles shyly. "It started out as a joke and, as happens with those who collect things, it took on a life of its own. My best friend and I have known each other since high school. When I confessed to her what I'd found out about Ben in our first year of marriage, she said someone needed to introduce him to something with a very pointy end." She walks to a framed drawing. "She got me this for our first anniversary to represent paper."

I cross the room to her and look closer. It is a beautiful pen and ink drawing of a bejeweled blade.

"For our second anniversary, this. The backing is cotton." She motions to an embroidered representation of a sword surrounded by roses.

Next, she motions to a leather thigh sheath with a small blade. "Leather is year three. Supposedly, it had been the property of some long-ago Scottish laird who had it made for his wife to wear under her skirts."

She continues to show me her collection. It went on, year after year, with gifts of blades of all kinds, a bronze spear, a wooden practice sword, ancient Chinese pottery with a spear motif, and even a gold necklace with a small knife pendant supplemented with an inset diamond.

"This one is my favorite," she says, pulling down an object from the wall. "On our eleventh anniversary, Monica gave me this beauty. It's a handcrafted Damascus blade with a jeweled hilt and matching sheath." She holds it out for me to inspect.

I whistle. I can't help it. This piece is beyond beautiful, it is gorgeous and opulent. The stones in the hilt catch the light and cast spears of color across the room.

"Ben hates them. He won't come in here, but I love them all," she whispers as she admires her collection.

"Locksmith?" I remind her. I carefully set the blade in its sheath on the corner of the desk.

"Oh, yes!" she says with a little bounce. "Where's my mind?" She picks up the cordless phone and looks at a card while dialing the number.

I inspect the wall of weaponry while she is on the phone. Every single piece is quite beautiful. Although I was startled at first, they make me think of Cait. Great to look at, but also with a bite that will make you sit up and take notice.

I sense that about her. Although she seems timid at times, I can tell she has a spine of steel. She has had to in order to put up with an ass like her husband for so long.

I have never understood men who can't see the value that is right in front of them and have to go sticking their dick in everything that catches their eye. It no longer matters if Cait is out of my league, not even a hundred million out of my league. I want her.

She hangs up the phone. "They can't come until tomorrow."

"Okay. I'll come back after my shift and sleep on your couch."

"Ford," she huffs. "There's no need for you to do that! I doubt Ben will return tonight. I think it scared him as much as it did me when he elbowed me. However, that may have only been because he heard the guard talking to the other officer on duty to call the police."

I turn and step to her, pleased that she doesn't back away from me when I invade her personal space. I look down into her eyes. They are a curious color that looks brown, but in the light have a golden hue, the tone of a very fine whisky.

"You don't know that for sure. You said yourself that he threatened to come back if you didn't make a deposit into his account, isn't that right?"

She looks down and away from me. I gently put my hand under her chin and tilt her face back up. "Look at me." When she does, I ask pointedly, "Did he or did he not threaten to come back?"

I hated to do it, but she needs to see that her husband may have taken a turn for the worse. His behavior last night could have been a trigger that pushed him to psychological places he hadn't gone before and once that line is crossed, it's easy for some people to stay on the other side of it. She has fire in her eyes and her lips are flattened in displeasure, but she nods.

My lips quirk. I like her feisty. With a mind of its own, my thumb does what it has wanted to do for a while and strokes across her bottom lip. A look of surprise transforms her face. Her eyes go wide, and those sexy lips part.

I shouldn't do it. My head is screaming stop, but I have to. Unable to change course, I lean down and kiss her. It's just a brush of my lips against hers.

I really want to bend her over the desk and pull down those silky pajama bottoms, lounge pants, or whatever the hell they are and fuck her until she comes all over my dick. That would be unwise, so I think better of it. If it has been twenty years since she's been with a man, I will need to slow down, to take it easy and not rush her.

"I've gotta go to work," I say, my voice gone rough, "but I'll be back after my shift. I'll either sleep on the couch or on your porch if you don't let me in. Your choice."

I stop in the doorway and look back at her stunned face. "And by the way, Cait, I love the new haircut." With that, I stride out of the room and back toward the front door, hoping I don't get lost in this maze of a house and ruin my grand exit.

Chapter 14

Caitlyn

I watch Ford strut out of the room after kissing me. He kissed me! I don't know whether to swoon or pitch a fit.

With two fingers, I touch my lips. They are still tingling from the touch of his. Maybe I'll swoon, just a teensy bit; I can't very well pitch a fit when he's already gone.

Not only had he kissed me, but he had also announced that he would be spending the night in my home or on my porch if I didn't let him in. What the actual hell? I barely know this man. Sure, he is an officer of the law, but that doesn't mean that he is above having nefarious intentions.

However, my instincts tell a different story. My instincts are telling me he is trustworthy. My hormones just want me to jump his bones. The trust part I can do.

The jumping the bones part, I wouldn't even know where to begin. If the fact that he kissed me is anything to go by, I might not have to do anything but enthusiastically join in when he jumps mine.

All right, now that I am reconciling myself to the fact that Ford will be staying in my house tonight, I need to decide where I am going to put him. In a house with six bedrooms, surely he could use one of them. I can't put him in any of the children's rooms and certainly not mine or the room Ben uses occasionally. That leaves one room, the room directly at the bottom of the stairs, which is directly below mine.

I try to remember to dust in that room every few weeks, but it has been a while. With there being potential showings, I should probably do a touch up, anyway. When I open the door, I am pleased to discover it isn't too bad. I open the windows to let some fresh air in, then go to retrieve the vacuum and a duster.

After dusting, vacuuming, and ensuring the attached bathroom is ready for a guest, I go to my room. Everything is in order there, too. Okay, that killed an hour.

I am not used to being sequestered in the house. I know I'm not really stuck here. Whenever I want, I can go out, but the thought of being seen with the evidence of Benjamin's anger plain on my face makes me cringe.

There's nothing for me to be ashamed of. It really had been an accident, but any attempts to explain it away would most likely have me branded as a battered wife who is living in delusion.

I hate that I wasn't able to work out this morning. Not going has messed up my whole routine.

Oh my goodness! I really am in a rut. One tiny disruption to my schedule and I feel like I am on pins and needles. What harm would it do to take a day off? Why can't I just be lazy and watch a movie or something?

I check the clock, wondering when Ford will be back. Remembering I have his card, I go to the office to retrieve it. Instead of potentially bothering him if he's in the middle of something, I send a less invasive text.

Ford, it's Cait. I'm sorry to bother you, but I was wondering when your shift normally ends. Don't eat before you come here.

I don't expect to hear from him right away, so I am surprised when my phone dings to let me know I have a message.

His response makes me smile. *Hey beautiful. Was just thinking about you. Usually around 6 but will let you know if something happens, and I get held up.*

Ford thinks I am beautiful. I should probably be leery of such a term of endearment coming from him when I barely know him, but I decide to just enjoy it. In my office, I sit at the desk and turn on the television, navigating to a favorite movie.

Because I've seen it several times, I don't need to pay close attention, so I power up my laptop. I type *Detective Ford Pickering OKC* into the search bar.

There isn't a lot of information about him in the results, just a few articles about cases he has been involved with. I take out his title and get a whole lot of nothing. Well, that's disappointing. I guess if I want to know more about him, I will have to just ask.

While I have my computer up, I send emails to my sons and ask when might be a good time to visit. Ben Jr. rarely responds, but I am still his mother and will keep reaching out to him until the day I die.

It saddens my heart how much he takes after his father. He is never satisfied, always looking for the greener grass over the next fence. I hope that someday he will find happiness, but he is grown now, and that's up to him.

I suddenly have the thought that I should let the attorney know what has happened. Locking Ben out of the house might not be a good idea even if he did give me a black eye, so I'd better get her take on it. I mute the television and take out Ms. Hartman's card.

When I hang up the phone, I immediately dial the locksmith and cancel the request. Without a court order, I can't lock Benjamin out of the house. According to the law, it is still his home, and he has as much right to access it as I do until I acquire a protective order.

She asked me about filing for one, but I told her to hold off for now. Ben has never been violent before and I have no reason to think that a simple accident has turned him into an abuser.

However, because of the non-profit for which I'm a board member, I know that abuse is a slippery slope and one incident can turn into regular abuse fairly quickly. Once a person breaks that boundary of hitting another, it's easier for them to do it again. I assure her that if anything happens to make me think he intends further violence that I will move forward with getting an order in place.

Ford can't stay in the house indefinitely, so there is no sense in him staying the night. Even if I found a house today and have enough money in my personal account to pay cash, it will still take some time before we could close, so I couldn't just move out.

Going to stay in a hotel wouldn't be ideal, either. That would also leave the house unattended. Who knows what Ben would do? I wonder if I could simply buy him out of his half of the house based upon the future sale.

Although the house's proceeds would revert to the trust, there are few restrictions for how I handle the funds. I could be a total bitch and give Benjamin nothing. However, if paying him out the half of the house he thinks he's owed would make him leave me alone, I'd be willing to do it.

I call the attorney back, apologizing for bothering her again, and ask if that is possible. She says that it is, but only if Ben agrees to it. Knowing he'd stay away, I could take my time finding just the right place to move to. I ask her to draw up a document with a few caveats I want to include.

She said she would try to have it to me later today, but since she is in court in the afternoon, it will probably be Monday. I hang up feeling better about this plan than simply locking him out.

I already have an appraisal scheduled for early next week. Once I have a value set from the appraiser and Ben's signature on the document, I will pay him the money out of the trust.

If he agrees, I will be able to end his access to the house. As much as I hate to give him any money because he's been such a lech, it is well worth a million or two to never have to sit across from him at breakfast again.

Starting today, I will go through the children's rooms and the rest of the house. I will pull out items that I want to take with me when I leave so that they can be boxed up and moved to storage in preparation for their new home.

I can also pull out any items that would be better off going to charity. First, I have to convince a certain detective that he doesn't need to spend the night. I go to the kitchen to make sure I have everything I need to do just that.

Chapter 15

Ford

It is nearly seven when I pull into Cait's driveway. I assume Ben hasn't shown his face since I didn't hear from her other than that single text that came in not long after I left this morning.

The whole calling her beautiful thing was probably a mistake. After an asshat like Ben, she is likely to be skittish. On the other hand, with an asshat like Ben, it has probably been a long time since someone has told her the truth.

When I'm parked, I reach into the back seat and take out the duffle bag I stopped by my place to pack. I only hope I don't have to fight her to get her to let me in. With one hand, I scrub my face before ringing the doorbell; this ongoing case is wearing me down.

When she opens the door, her face is flushed. The sight of the bruise around her eye pisses me off all over again and part of me hopes her jerk husband shows up tonight.

"Oh good, it's you!" she says. "I just took dinner out of the oven. Please, come in."

Well, that was easy.

I close the door behind me and watch her walk back toward the kitchen. She is wearing some black pants that hug her curves nicely. She has a great round ass. Those pants look stretchy, so they'd probably be easy to slide off.

Her ass disappears as she turns around. When she looks at me and sees where my eyes had been, she looks behind her and back at me, raising her eyebrows. "I said," she says with amusement dancing in her eyes, "would you like something to drink?"

"Uh, yeah, sure."

Great comeback Shakespeare.

"I have beer, wine, water, milk, or I may still have some pop down in the kids' playroom," she goes on, turning back toward the kitchen.

I drop my duffel on a sofa as we pass through the living room. "Beer would be good."

"Stout or pale?"

"Stout if you've got it," I say.

"Oh, I've got it," she replies, pulling a cold bottle out of a glass front refrigerator.

She twists it open and pours it expertly into a chilled glass. "A friend's son started up a brewery a few years ago," she explains. "They were struggling with capital, so I gave them a couple of small infusions that carried them through. It got the brewery off the ground soon enough and it's doing well now. Every few weeks, they bring me fresh beer."

"Nice," I say, taking a drink. "Wow, that's smooth."

She grins at me. "I know. I had to taste everything before I made the investment. They have a real flair for flavor."

My stomach growls, which is embarrassing, but she's the one who told me not to eat before coming here. "Something smells great."

"I hope you're a meat and potatoes kind of guy. I was in the mood for comfort food. Do you mind if we eat in the kitchen? I'm afraid I've got the dining table covered with stuff."

"No, that's fine. Do you mind if I change into something more comfortable? It's been a long day, and I'd like to just relax."

"Oh! Certainly!" She looks flustered. "There's a bathroom just down the hall to the right."

"Great. Thanks. I'll be right back."

With a detour back to the living room, I grab my duffel, then go to find the bathroom Cait indicated. I left my jacket at home when I'd stopped by, but hadn't wanted to change into something super casual until I'd seen how she was dressed.

I could see myself showing up in a pair of sweats to find her dressed to the nines for dinner. The ways of rich people are beyond me. I get the impression Cait's not snooty, but I really don't know her that well.

I'm glad she feels comfortable enough with me to be relaxed. Just thinking about her round ass in those stretchy pants makes my dick twitch. I'm going to have to stop thinking about her like that or I'll be jumping her before dinner is over.

When I remove my shield and holster from my belt, I set them on the counter, then pull off my dress shirt. The tee I have on under my dress shirt comes off, too. I've had it on all day, and it smells of stale coffee and sweat. I turn on the tap and inspect myself in the mirror.

Good looking is not a descriptor I ever assigned to myself, but I don't think I'm bad looking either. I may be a little worse for wear after forty some-odd years on the planet, including the last twenty-eight as a cop, but that's to be expected.

There's a little more gray hair at my temples and sprinkled about, but I don't much care. Getting older is a fact of life and there is no sense denying it.

My muscles aren't as prominent as they'd been when I was younger, but I'm not in bad shape. I also don't have what my nieces call a Dad-bod either.

Although a lot of my co-workers let themselves go over time, getting soft isn't an option for me. There are still times when I have to chase down some perp and if I was fat enough for it to affect my reflexes, it could cost someone their life.

Once the tap is warm, I bend and splash my face, trying to rinse away the dregs of the day. The cold beer and promise of a good meal have already gone a long way toward accomplishing that. The fact that there is a beautiful woman waiting for me in the other room is just icing on the cake.

I dry my face and wonder if maybe I should have taken the time to shave off the scruff. Then I think about Cait waiting for me and decided I've taken enough time. I pull on a pair of gray sweatpants and an OKCPD t-shirt, leaving my shoes off, choosing to go barefoot as Cait is.

She has tiny feet; it seems to me. Before my tired mind can be diverted down that rabbit trail, I tuck everything back into the duffle and leave it in the bathroom, then go back toward the kitchen.

She's waiting for me when I come back. She has a couple of plates on the counter, along with a roast with potatoes and carrots on a tray. "Are you picky? If so..."

"I'm not picky, Cait," I tell her. "I'll eat just about anything."

She hesitates before she starts putting food onto a plate. I wonder what thoughts she is having that would cause her to pause like that. She dishes out a healthy portion of everything before handing me the plate.

"There are place settings on the table along with rolls and butter," she says, nodding to a small table tucked into an alcove off the kitchen.

She has moved my beer to the table, too, giving me the seat in the corner against the wall. It is just where I would have seated myself. From that position, I have a good view out the adjacent window and down the hall, back toward the living room.

When she readies her own plate, she comes to sit across from me carrying a glass of wine with her. I waited for her to sit before reaching for a roll and buttering it.

"You said your father was religious, are you?"

"No," she replies, divining my implication, "I don't say grace over my meals, so please, dig in."

I take a bite and groan. "It's been a long time since I've had food this good."

She flushes with pleasure at the compliment. "I've enjoyed cooking today. I don't do it very often anymore since it's just me here most of the time. It's not really worth the mess to cook for one."

"Same here. Not that I could make anything close to this good, though. If it can't be thrown onto a grill, it's out of my wheelhouse."

"So, Detective Pickering, you got to hear all about my life story and dirty laundry, but I know almost nothing about you. What made you decide to be a police officer?"

"I've wanted to be one for as long as I can remember. When I was a kid, I loved mystery novels and puzzles. I watched all the cop shows on television - Hill Street Blues, TJ Hooker, even Cagney and Lacey. I couldn't get enough of it."

"How long have you been a police officer?"

"Since I was twenty. I got a job as a patrol officer when I was three quarters of the way through a criminal justice degree at OSU. I was able to finagle my courses around my shift enough to finish out the degree before I had a year on the job."

"And a detective?" she asks.

"I made the move from Stillwater to OKCPD after two years in Stilly, then I moved up after I'd been on the job for four more years. I made the rounds through the various areas until I landed in homicide. It suited me, so I've been there since."

"I can't imagine how hard that must be to see the worst that people can do to one another every day," she shudders with the statement.

"It can be tough. But I'm pretty good at stopping them from doing it again," I say.

She focuses on her plate and says quietly, "Have you ever been married?"

"I was once," I tell her. "Right before I moved to the City, I married my college sweetheart and brought her with me. She hated it here and hated the life of being married to a cop. We were only married for a couple of years before she called it quits and went back home. After that, there were a couple of long-term relationships, but nothing stuck to the point where we were ready to get married."

Some spouses can't handle the worry that goes with the job. Some can't handle the fact that they spend a lot of time alone with their partner working long hours and being called out at all hours of the day and night as duty requires, then returning home too exhausted to do anything.

I don't blame my ex-wife for leaving. She got remarried to a great guy who is the manager at one of those big home supply stores. They have four kids and she is happy.

"Do you have any children?"

I shake my head. "No. That's probably my only regret about not having a marriage that stuck. However, I have nieces and nephews galore, and I love to spoil them rotten."

"How many siblings do you have?"

"I have three sisters and a brother. My brother and one of my sisters live in Oklahoma; she's in Tulsa and he's here in the City. My other two sisters live in the Dallas metro."

That gets a smile out of her. "I always wondered what it would be like to have siblings. I was an only child of only children, so besides my own children, I don't have much family. Do you want some more?"

The question surprises me. I follow her gaze down to my plate, which is empty and practically wiped clean with one of the rolls.

"There's plenty," she says, "but I also have dessert, so keep that in mind."

I perk at that. A wicked sweet tooth is something I've never been able to shake. "I think I'll save the rest of my room for dessert. The meal was delicious, Cait."

She takes my plate along with hers to the sink, then pulls out two smaller plates from a cabinet. She lifts a glass top off a cake pedestal that I hadn't noticed.

"This is a chocolate mayonnaise cake that my Mama used to make. It was always one of my favorites," she tells me as she slices a wedge and puts it onto a plate for me.

"Mayonnaise, huh? I can't say I've ever had a cake made with mayonnaise," I say skeptically.

She laughs at me. "Trust me, you'll like it. The mayonnaise just makes it really moist." She places the plate in front of me with a fresh fork.

I wait for her to sit down again with a piece of her own before I dare a bite. She watches me cut a piece and take a bite. As I close my eyes to chew, I catch a glimpse of her smile before she starts eating.

I swallow and look across the table at her. "My God, woman, if you weren't married, I'd marry you just for your cake."

She barks out a laugh as I'd hoped she would. Then she grows serious.

Looking at her plate, she says, "When I talked to my attorney today, she said I can't lock Benjamin out of his home without a court order, so I canceled the appointment with the locksmith."

"I was afraid of that," I reply.

"However, I have come up with a plan that may satisfy him and, if he agrees, he will move all of his things out. Then I will be able to change the locks and he will no longer have access to the house. We'll still be married, but living completely separate."

As she speaks, I watch her moving the cake on her plate around with her fork. She's worried. I wish I had a way to take her worry away, but I can only do so much based on the short time we've known each other. I can't exactly go all caveman, knock her on the head, and drag her off to my cave to keep her safe.

"Do you think he will agree?" I ask.

She shrugs. "I hope so. Getting an infusion of a large sum of cash will be attractive to him if his actions last night are anything to go by. My attorney is working on an angle to break the prenup. If she can do that, I'll finally be free. She just needs some time. As I'm sure you know, the courts don't always work swiftly. But," she says, rising from her chair, "I've been waiting for twenty-five years; what's a few more months?"

She goes to the sink and scrapes her mostly uneaten cake into the sink. She rinses the plate and the others, then puts them into the dishwasher. I get up to help her put things away.

"Anyway," she says after working in silence for some time, "there's really no need for you to stay the night here. I really doubt he'll be back."

I stop her hands from working and take them in mine. She is shaking.

"Cait," I say, waiting for her to look at me before I go on, "there's no harm in me staying one night. I put my car back by the garage so that it can't be seen from the street. If he comes in, I'll be here. You don't have to be afraid."

"I don't want to be. Never in my life did I think he would hurt me, but he was so angry last night."

I pull her into my arms. "It's okay. You're not alone in this anymore. I'm here with you."

She lets out a weak laugh against my chest. "You don't even know me."

"Sure, I do," I say against her hair. She feels so good in my arms. "Like you said, I know your life story and all your dirty laundry. I probably know more about you than some of your friends."

"That's true. Only Monica knows more than you," she replies, her voice muffled by my shirt.

"Monica of the weapons wall?"

"The very same."

I feel her chest expand in my arms as she takes a deep breath. She lets it out and pulls away from me.

"Better?" I ask, cupping her cheek with my hand.

She nods. "Yes, thank you."

Chapter 16

Caitlyn

S omething came over me and I just started to feel shaky when I told Ford he didn't need to stay. I guess I hadn't realized how afraid I really was. It's a strange feeling for me to need someone after learning years ago to be almost completely self-reliant, particularly when it came to managing my own emotions and needs.

Now I am standing here with Ford's hand on my cheek, looking up into those deep, dark, soulful eyes, and I feel shaky for a completely different reason. Instead of icy fear overcoming me, heat begins to build.

I see it coming. He gives me time to stop it, but I don't want to stop it. His head lowers. I take in a breath, hoping to quell my nerves. His mouth finds mine with a sweet brushing of lips.

He kisses me as he had this morning, but this time he lingers. The brush of lips becomes a press. His tongue licks against my lips and a thrill surges through me. I open for him, his tongue touching and teasing mine, drawing it into the dance.

His mouth tastes of chocolate and the pungent hops of the beer, a heady combination. He smells slightly of sweat overlaid by his lingering aftershave and the intoxicating smell of man.

He pulls my body against his and I feel myself melt against him as I snake my arms around his neck. It has been so long since someone has held me like this, and it feels so damn good I think I might cry.

The surge of emotions is overwhelming. I am grateful, nervous, peaceful, scared, content, and so turned on I don't know what to do with it all.

I feel his erection growing against my stomach. Apparently, I am not the only one turned on. I feel embarrassment swamp me. It's like I'm an eighteen-year-old inexperienced girl again. The little bit of experience I have from relations with Ben is nothing to go on, and I don't know what to do or how to react, so I do nothing but keep kissing him.

He growls against my mouth, then stoops to grasp my butt and pull me up. When he sits me on the counter, he wedges himself between my legs. They spread wide for him, and he presses his erection against my center.

I feel like lightning has struck me. The connection makes my body sizzle from head to toe. Being with Ben never made me feel this way; not even close.

Ford stops abruptly, pulling his mouth from mine. He puts his hands on the counter on each side of me and lowers his head to my shoulder. "I don't want to rush you," he says, his voice is sonorous and full of strain.

I pull my arms from his neck and circle his torso, rubbing his back. "I was really enjoying the kissing part," I tell him honestly.

"But..."

"I don't know. It's been a long time for me. I haven't been with anyone since Ben."

The feel of his body is incredible, and I love the way I feel when I am with him. However, this is all moving way too fast.

A week ago, I didn't even know this man's name, but that first time we met, the spark of attraction was undeniable. I've been enamored, and it is so out of left field I don't know what to do with it.

"Over twenty years ago," he recalls.

"Yes," I confirm. "But I've also never felt this strong of a sexual attraction before. It frightens me a little."

He lets out a breath. "Okay. We'll slow it down. Like I said, I don't want to rush you, from the moment I first saw you, I wanted you, but I understand where you're coming from. I like you, Cait, and I am incredibly attracted to you, too. However, I think there is the potential for something more here and the last thing I want to do is jeopardize the future by rushing the present."

Did he really say what I think he said just now? I feel a little flutter at the idea that he is as attracted to me as I am to him. If he is being honest, I can too.

"I think I felt the same way," I breathe. "I didn't realize it at the time because, well, I'd never felt like that before, so I had nothing to compare it to."

"Don't tell me things like that or I won't be able to slow down," he grouses.

I laugh.

"Is it okay if I shower in the bathroom you had me change in?" he asks. "I need a cold one."

I laugh again. "No."

He looks up at me before I can finish. "What?"

I shake my head. "No, you don't need to use that shower. Since you're intent on staying here tonight, I prepared a room for you. Let me show you where, so that you can get set up in there. You can shower or do whatever else you need to in there."

"Oh, okay. After I shower, I want you to show me around this place so I have a better lay of the land," he says.

"I can do that."

He kisses me again before cupping my butt and pulling me down from the counter. Once I am standing on my own two feet again, I turn to lead him to the bedroom I'd aired out this morning.

He keeps my hand in his as we make our way down the hall. It's sweet. I like it. Like it a lot.

I show him into the room, and after another quick kiss, leave him to his own devices. Going back to the kitchen, I finish putting the remains of our dinner away.

The padding of his feet carries into the kitchen as he retrieves his belongings from the guest bath and goes back toward the front of the house and his bedroom.

I start the tablet I keep in the kitchen for recipes and start some music. The elation I'm feeling is something I want to hold on to and make last as long as possible. I just made out with a man.

Oh, my God! I just made out with a man!!!

Kissing a man that isn't my husband might be the fast track to hell, but I can't bring myself to care. I touch my lips. They are still tender and tingly from Ford's kisses, and I want to do that some more.

Everything is put away and I am wiping down the counters when I catch a movement in the corner of my eye. "Hey!" I turn and say brightly, thinking it's Ford.

But it isn't Ford. Benjamin stands in the doorway to the kitchen, and he is seething. His clothes are rumpled, and his eyes are bloodshot. If I hadn't just seen him last night, I would wonder if he had been on a three-day bender.

It has been a long time since he has shown up here in that state. Threats of withholding the extra money I gave him had him straightening up quickly. The last time that happened was over five years ago.

When we met, Ben was handsome and charming. He dressed well and kept himself impeccably groomed. Over the years, he has steadily gone downhill.

"I told you I would be back if you didn't transfer my goddamn money," he grits out.

Lifting my chin in defiance, I say, "I don't have a penny of your money. The monthly amount you've been receiving was something I did out of the kindness of my heart. Well, I don't have any more of that left for you and, according to my attorney, I'm not obligated to continue."

Where is Ford? Maybe he is still in the shower and didn't hear Benjamin come in. If so, I need to stall.

"Your attorney? Did that old man finally grow some balls?" Ben sneers at me.

I don't feel obligated to correct his assumption. Ben is good at assuming things. "I'm not giving you a monthly allowance any longer, so you'll just have to learn to live on your salary."

"What about the house? You're selling it, but your father gave it to both of us."

"See, that's the thing about my father. You had to pay close attention to how he worded things. The house is owned by the trust and he was only allowing both of us the use of it. You've stopped using it. I'm the only one who lives here full time, and it's too much for one person, so yes, as trustee, I'm selling it. The proceeds will go back into the trust."

"Then where will you live? If you buy another house with the trust's money, I'll have just as much right to have access to it, too." He is still sneering.

I shouldn't have done it. That look of condescension on his face and the desire to wipe it off pushed me over the edge and I forgot all about keeping my cards close to my chest. I probably should have kept my big mouth shut, but he was looking so smug, like I was too stupid to know anything about anything.

"I will be buying a house with my own money, and you won't have the right to access squat."

"What money?" he guffaws. "You don't have any of your own money. You've never worked a day in your life."

As if raising three children wasn't work. However, he wouldn't know, would he? He was never around when our children were growing up. "Unlike you, I didn't spend every penny of my allowance."

He steps forward, radiating menace. "If you think you can fuck me over on this house, you've got another thing coming." He freezes, his eyes going wide.

"Keep making threats like that and I'll throw your ass in lockup." Ford growls. "Go on into the kitchen and let's have a civilized conversation."

Benjamin takes a few more steps into the kitchen and I see that Ford's gun is against the back of Ben's head. When he steps in, I lose my breath because the only thing Ford has on is a towel wrapped around his hips. His hair is wet and dripping, but he is clean shaven, so that must be what had delayed his shower.

Ford takes his gun away from Ben's head and Ben spins around to get a good look at the man with the gun. "Who the fuck are you?" Ben barks at Ford and without allowing him time to answer, he turns to me and asks incredulously, "Are you fucking this guy?"

I lift my chin again after picking it up off the floor because it had fallen there upon getting a good look at Ford in that towel. There might still be a little drool I need to mop up.

"Not that it's any of your business, but no, I have not had sex with him."

Yet.

Ford gives me a lecherous smile, as if he is reading my mind. When Ben turns back to him, Ford's face is stone again.

"I am a friend of your wife's Mr. Foster. When I found out about the assault last night and the threat to return today, I didn't want her staying alone."

"Friend, huh? Big man with a gun," Ben taunts. "How about I call the cops and tell them there's an intruder in my home?"

"Go ahead," Ford says with a smile full of razor wire. "You can tell them the intruder's name is Detective Ford Pickering with the Oklahoma City Police Department."

Call me petty, but it gives me a thrill of satisfaction to see Ben blanch at Ford's statement. Then Ford's previous words must have sunk in.

"Assault?" Ben gasps. "There was no assault. It was an accident." He turns to me, looking angry again. "You told them I assaulted you?"

I start to respond, but Ford gives his head a subtle shake to indicate I shouldn't. My mouth closes firmly.

"Mr. Foster," Ford says calmly, "I strongly advise you to refrain from making threats against your wife. She's not alone for you to push around anymore. Based upon your history, I would say she has been more than generous to you, and you have no room to complain."

He pauses to move slightly forward so that he is almost between Ben and me.

"However, should you decide that you have been legally wronged by Cait, get yourself an attorney and take it up with the court system. If there are any more threats or any other form of harassment, I will personally see to it that you are arrested. She has permission to call me at any time, and my precinct is only a few miles away."

Ben huffs and turns on his heel. "Good luck with getting her into bed. She's as frigid as they come, or don't cum, as was the case with her."

His words sting. I feel as if he's slapped me.

"Can't say as I blame her," Ford says. "If I had a husband who went around sticking his dick in everything that moved, I wouldn't want him in my bed, either."

Ben just glares at me before he stomps out of the kitchen and back toward the front door. Ford follows him out to make sure he leaves.

There are some noises I can't identify, then a few minutes later, Ford comes back, dressed in sweats and a t-shirt again. Damn, I'd hoped he was still in just a towel. He has also put his gun away.

He makes a beeline to me, cupping my face and tilting it up. He looks at me for a long moment, assessing. "You okay?"

I nod, putting my hand over his and leaning into the touch. "Thank you." I throw my arms around him. "I'm so glad you were here."

He wraps me up, cradling my head with one hand and patting my back with the other. "I am, too. That guy's a real asshole."

I choke out a laugh against his chest.

"So," he says. "What's next?"

I look up at him and smooth my hand down his cheek. "You look like you've had a long day."

"I have," he says, "but I'm not out of juice yet."

"You said you wanted to see the rest of the house," I remind him.

"Yep. Lead the way."

By the time I finish showing him all three floors, I can tell he is exhausted and trying not to let me see him yawn. When we make it back down to the main floor, I stop at the door to his bedroom.

"I can tell you're exhausted. Go to bed and I'll see you in the morning."

His head drops forward. "I'm sorry, Cait."

"What on earth do you have to be sorry for?"

"I'm sorry I'm crashing on you," he says.

"Ford, you've worked hard all week long. You have a hard job that takes a toll on your body and your mind. When you need rest, you need to take it. Go to bed."

I lean up and kiss his cheek. He goes into his assigned room and I go upstairs to bed. I toss and turn, unable to sleep.

There is an amazingly hot man downstairs who thinks I'm beautiful. Part of me wants to throw caution to the wind, but over two decades of inaction is throwing a giant glass of cold water on the whole shebang.

Even if I did go down there, I don't know that I'm ready for sex. Yet. I need to stop thinking about this. I need to calm down and go to sleep.

I could pull out my vibrator and give myself a release. After all, instead of some made up masculine idea, there is a real-world man with dark brown eyes who kisses like the devil himself sleeping downstairs that can provide plenty of fantasy fuel.

I wonder if Ford is sleeping any better than I. Probably, I tell myself. He looked so tired when we parted ways.

A crazy idea seeps into my head and won't let go. I push out of bed and make my way downstairs. I'll just knock on the door quietly and if he doesn't answer, that will mean he's fast asleep. His door isn't closed. It's standing wide open. I pause in the hallway, suddenly unsure of myself.

This is crazy. Let the man have his rest.

I turn to go back upstairs.

"Cait?" he says, his voice sleepy.

"Sorry," I say quietly, "I didn't mean to wake you."

"What is it?"

"I just...I...I'm sorry. It's silly. I shouldn't have bothered you."

"Cait," he says, his voice firm.

I sigh. "I was just wondering if I could maybe sleep with you. Not for like sex or anything, it's just been...I hate sleeping alone in this mausoleum."

He moves under the covers, then holds them up, inviting me in. "C'mon."

I cross the room quickly and practically dive under the covers with him. I expect to just lay there in bed with him, but his muscular arm goes around my waist, and he pulls me against his body, my back to his front.

His scent surrounds me, comforts me, and makes me feel safe, and my inability to sleep dissipates as soon as my head settles on the pillow.

Chapter 17

Caitlyn

I wake the next morning and realize I'm not in my bed. My pulse starts to rocket when memories of the night before swim to the surface. I slept with Ford last night. A smile curls my lips.

I hear a razor buzzing in the bathroom, so I get out of bed and go upstairs. In my bathroom, I run a comb through my hair, brush my teeth, wash my face, and put on something other than the pajamas I wore to bed. When I return downstairs, I start coffee brewing.

It felt really, really good sleeping with Ford. No, good isn't a strong enough word. It was flipping fantastic.

For a man to be able to do that with no expectations of anything else is astounding to me. I hear the stories from my girlfriends about their boyfriends and husbands, heck, the stories of my own husband, who are driven by their baser urges, claiming they can't help themselves.

They take what they want without care of what their partner needs. Once it's over, they're all promises and apologies, swearing that it won't happen again. Next time, they'll take their time, use more care. It always seems to happen again.

Ford appears to be that ultimate of rare creatures—a truly honorable man. Of course, I will be the first to admit that the male influences in my life have been incredibly abysmal, leaving me with a skewed view.

I have a few male acquaintances that seem to be honorable, but I only see what's on the surface. Who knows what's lingering underneath?

As if my thoughts of him conjure him, Ford comes into the kitchen dressed in his sweats and tee again. He's freshly shaved and clean faced.

He kisses me on the cheek, which makes my heart lurch. "Is that coffee I smell?" he asks.

"Yes," I answer, "it's just about ready. Do you want some breakfast?"

"Is there any more of that casserole you gave me yesterday?"

"Yes, or I can make you something fresh."

"You could feed me that casserole every day for the rest of my life and I would be a cheerful man."

"You're easy," I say.

He looks at me with a wicked grin and says, "You have no idea."

I laugh at his comment. To see that he can be silly warms my heart. It has to be difficult to remain light-hearted when so much of his life at work must be serious and filled with darkness.

I serve him up a plate of food and cup of coffee much like I did yesterday morning, only this time, I eat with him.

"What's on your agenda for today?" he asks.

"I have items stacked up in the dining room that I need to get ready for storage to prepare for selling the house. My realtor is hoping to show it to someone who may want to buy it along with all the contents. That will be fantastic, but I'll need to have anything I want to keep out of the house before they come to look at it. *If* they come look at it."

"I'm available to help."

"Ford, why would you want to do a bunch of manual labor on your day off? You should be spending the day at home relaxing."

"With two of us, it will get done quickly and then we can both relax," he says.

There was nothing quick about it, but with two of us, we did get everything packed and to the storage facility in a day. It's late in the day, but we're still done in one. It would have taken me all weekend just to pack and several trips next week to get it all to storage.

I'm not ready for him to leave when we're done, so I ply him with the best of my womanly wiles. That's right, I offer him good food and great beer followed by excellent chocolate cake.

We've spent all day talking about our families and friends. It has felt good to get to know more about each other and was probably a good idea after sleeping in the same bed with him last night.

I turn on some music as we clean up and put things away. I like the channel because it's one that plays a variety of music. It doesn't take long for us to be bopping and singing along when we know the words.

A slow song comes on and Ford comes up to me, takes me in his arms and sways with me. He's wearing jeans and a different t-shirt today, which makes me wonder if he packed enough clothes for a few days.

He smells fantastic, like hops from the beer he's been drinking, soap, and just a hint of cinnamon. The smell wraps around me, and I relax against him.

When we find our groove with me swaying along with him, he moves us around the kitchen. He's crooning the words he knows. Words about dancing barefoot in the grass. Words of love and how the singer thinks his woman, his person, his angel, looks so perfect to him.

The song ends and moves on to something more upbeat, but Ford holds me, still swaying. I really, really want him to kiss me...a lot. I'd like to make out with him like we did last night on the counter.

Be brave, Cait.

"I think I'd really like to make out with you," I say, "but I don't want to be... What's it called? A tease? Yeah, I don't want to be a tease and get you all worked up when there might not be the big payoff."

He chuckles. "Well, I certainly appreciate that. While we worked today, I was thinking about it, your, our situation, I mean. I want you. I want to make that very clear. But I understand that it's almost like you're starting all over again physically and emotionally and, based upon my impression of your husband, he probably wasn't the best representation of lovemaking."

He's right. I don't hate sex, but after being with Benjamin a few times, I wondered what all the fuss was about. It wasn't horrible, but it wasn't particularly fun or pleasurable either.

"Okay."

"So, I think it's going to work best if I let you lead and that we communicate a lot until you're comfortable. That way, if you want to make out, I'll let you instigate and if it starts to go too fast or too far and you're not ready for that, you can put on the brakes, and we'll stop."

I look up at him with furrowed brows. "That doesn't sound very fair to you."

He chuckles again. "It's my idea, Darlin. And I am confident that you are worth it. So, do you want to make out on the kitchen counter again?" He asks with a wolfish grin.

That makes me laugh, which is what he intended, I think. "We can start there. That seemed to work out well for us last night."

"Yes, it did," he says and boosts me up on the counter again. He studies my face, smoothing my hair back.

"You are so damn beautiful. You don't know this, but you were the reason I joined that gym. I saw you when I visited and thought it was a good sign. My old schedule had me at odds with your visits until things shifted about a month ago. I'm glad it changed because you would have been gone and I never would have known where you went."

He thinks I'm beautiful. No man has said that to me since I was nineteen and looking back, I doubt Benjamin meant it. He thought my father's money was beautiful. Me, not so much.

"It must have been fate," I say, instead of gushing about the fact that he thinks I'm beautiful.

"Sure seems like it."

"Now, where were we?" I ask, putting a hand on his cheek.

Chapter 18

Ford

I am wakened by the buzzing of my phone on the nightstand. For a moment, I'm disoriented, but then the amazing creature next to me mumbles in protest. Cait. My beautiful Cait.

She might not like me saying she's mine, but it's the truth. I was drawn to her from the first time I saw her and even though she's not completely free to be mine yet, she will be soon.

That arrogant asshole of a husband is an idiot to have taken her for granted. The fact that he cheated on her is beyond my capacity to understand.

He called her frigid. My experience with her is about as far from frigid as she could be. I don't know what he was doing with her, but any frigidity was because of him and not her.

She is about as hot as hot can get. I had to work hard to keep a straight face sometimes. It was as if she was experiencing some things for the very first time. There were several times when a look of surprised excitement crossed her face like when she did that bit with the flick of her tongue after taking my shirt off, well...I've never seen anything as adorable as that and it made me want to laugh.

I extricate myself from her, trying to disturb her as little as possible. She mumbles something else, then turns away and snuggles down into her pillow. I take the phone to the bathroom, so the light doesn't wake her.

Of course, it's work. Another dead body. Another despicable action by one human being against another.

I hate to leave Cait, but I have a job to do. I know she understands; she seems to understand better than most, but that doesn't make it any easier. If I had my way, I'd crawl back into that bed with her and wake up with her in the morning.

I quickly pack up my things and throw on some clothes. I've exhausted the clothes I brought with me, so I'll need to repack before I come back. If she wants me to come back, that is.

I send a text giving them an ETA for my arrival. I'll need to go by my place to shower and put on a suit before going to the crime scene. I should have brought a suit with me, but I didn't want to be presumptuous.

Once I'm packed up, I go back into the bedroom, leaving the bathroom light on but shutting the door most of the way. I sit on the bed and shake Cait gently.

"Cait..." I say, my voice low.

She wakes with a start. "What?"

"Shhh...I just wanted to let you know I have to go to work."

She reaches out a hand and puts it on my thigh. "Oh, okay," she says, her voice muzzy from sleep. "Be safe."

That's it. Be safe. No fuss, no histrionics, just quiet acceptance. It's the first time, though. I wonder if she will be as accepting when it's the hundredth.

It may be only because she's half asleep, but her quiet acceptance that I'm getting called in is a relief. My work can be difficult for others to accept. Even my family has had to adjust to me being called out in the middle of a dinner or birthday party.

I lean over and kiss her. "I will, Darlin. I'll call you when I can."

"Mmmm..." she mumbles something else, but I can't make it out. She's halfway back to dreamland already.

I turn the lock on the knob as I go out the front door. I can't lock the deadbolt, but the person most likely to come in and do her harm has a key.

She said she has a plan for that and I'm just hoping it works out the way she hopes it does. However, if it doesn't, maybe me putting a gun to the back of his head will make him think twice before trying to bully her again, or worse.

"What do we have?" I ask the officer at the door of the convenience store when I arrive at the scene.

"Triple homicide," he says, "three male victims that appear to be the owner and his two sons. Register is open, so it could be a robbery gone wrong."

"Thanks," I tell him and enter the store. The scene is a mess, but the techs are already on-site cataloging everything. One of them approaches me and says there's video in a small office in the back of the storage room. I follow him to view the recordings.

A lot of detectives fall into their roles with no forethought or planning. It just seems like a logical step up the ladder in their career progression. From the beginning, I wanted to be a detective and, specifically, a homicide detective.

I've worked hard to gain and hone the skills that make for an excellent investigator. Although it can be frustrating when a case goes cold or when it becomes bogged down in bureaucratic red tape, I try to focus on the cases I can push forward toward a resolution and conviction. The successes help me keep working those stalled cases without getting overwhelmed with the lack of progress and burned out.

I focus on the current scene and begin to compile the details and clues. It's a piece of the puzzle and all the pieces need to be fit together to form a cohesive picture. I hate that the lives of three human beings have been snuffed out in a senseless act, but my thrill at the chase will hopefully bring justice for their loved ones.

It was still dark outside when I arrived at the crime scene in the wee hours of the morning. I leave several hours later to find the sun pushing its way through the horizon, casting a riot of colors across the sky. There's nothing more to do at the moment except wait for the techs to finish and go through their findings.

I pull my phone out. My first impulse is to call, but it's still quite early, so maybe a text is better.

Me: *Good morning darlin. Sorry, I wasn't there to say it in person.*

I'm surprised when my phone buzzes right away with a response.

Cait: *I missed waking up to you, but I understand that you're needed. Will I see you today?*

Me: *Yes. Just leaving the scene and nothing else to be done right now. The waiting game begins.*

Cait: *Breakfast?*

Me: *On my way.*

I put my phone away with a smile.

"What are you grinning about?" my partner, Jim Bergen, asks.

"Nothing. Just thinking about breakfast."

"Breakfast makes you that happy, huh?" He observes as he pulls out a cigarette and lights it.

"When it's with a beautiful woman, it does."

"Beautiful woman? When did this come about?"

"Recently."

I don't elaborate. My private life is private, and I've always made a point of keeping it that way. Not that I've had much of a private life outside of work and family. Even so, I've never been one that has felt the need to share every little thing with others. The thought of family reminds me I'm supposed to have lunch today with my brother that lives here in the City.

It's a regular standing family meal, but I always try to go if I can make it. I wonder if Cait will go with me. If not, I may skip it. I can understand that Cait might not be ready for the whole meet the family routine.

I know it's all very new, but it doesn't feel that way. It feels as if Cait has stepped into an open space in my life that was made just for her. It's hard to believe that it's only been a few days.

Chapter 19

Caitlyn

It only takes a slight tilt of my head to kiss him. Shyly at first, but as the connection is made, it deepens.

Making out with Ford has been a revelation. With Benjamin, the first time we French kissed reminded me of trying to kiss a boat propeller. His tongue was like a whirling dervish once it touched mine, and I didn't find that sexy at all.

All of this comparing might not be a good thing for me to do, but with my limited frame of reference, I can't seem to stop. Everything I had thought of as reality is being completely thrown out the window.

My whole paradigm is shifting. I never missed sex and only occasionally used my vibrator when I felt a strong need for release.

However, with Ford, just making out with him on this kitchen counter is setting my whole body on fire with desire. He's only kissing me, and I am so turned on I want to rip his clothes off and take him inside me right now. My mind conjures the vision of him in only a towel in this very room.

I need more skin. There are too many clothes in the way. My hands pull at the hem of his shirt, and it comes off easily once we break our mouths apart.

I'm breathing hard. The sight of the broad expanse of hard chest, smattered with dark hair, inflames me even more. I just stare at it for a long moment before I reach my hands up and drag my nails across all that bare man flesh. He hisses in response.

I notice his nipples harden and can't help myself from leaning forward and flicking one with the tip of my tongue. The groan that escapes him sends a thrill through me. Never have I felt so powerful.

I look up at him. I don't know what he sees on my face, but his mouth crashes back into mine as his hands grip my hips and pull me to the edge of the counter where he presses against me. His constrained erection grinds against my core, tipping me into a frenzied madness that I've never felt before.

My legs go around his waist, pulling him harder against me. It's not enough. I pull away from him. "I need more," I say breathlessly.

"Tell me what you need, Darlin."

"More," I reply, unable to think clearly through the haze of lust.

He cups my jaw and turns my face up. "Darlin, you're driving, remember? Tell me what you need."

His sonorous voice cuts through the haze and settles me. "There are too many clothes in the way."

He smiles, and it is beautiful. "That's easily remedied." He starts to pull up my shirt.

When I notice where we are and remember the wall of windows behind us, I grab the hem of my shirt and stop him from pulling it off. "Wait! Not here," I say, looking over my shoulder.

He understands and helps me down from the countertop. Taking me by the hand, he leads me into the bedroom he's been using. He stops a few feet from the bed and turns to me, leaning down to kiss my forehead.

Gently, he puts a hand on each of my forearms and lifts my arms over my head. In one swift movement, he pulls my shirt off.

I lower my arms and rest my hands on his shoulders as he reaches around and unfastens my bra. His lips trail kisses along the top of one shoulder as he carefully removes it.

He pulls back and looks down at me. With his large hands, he cups my bare breasts as if testing their weight. His thumbs stroke across my nipples in tandem, leaving hard peaks in their wake.

Unease uncoils in my belly as I remember the sag in my breasts. My hands tighten on his shoulders as I try not to focus on the fact of what he's seeing.

His hands mold and reshape my breasts. I'm sure he notices how soft and yielding they are. Breastfeeding takes away the firmness of your boobs rather quickly.

He moves his hands down my sides, stroking over the roundness of my flesh. His fingers grip the waist of my pants as he lowers himself, planting more kisses down my breastbone, between my breasts, down to the paunch of my belly.

He pulls my pants down over my hips, down my thighs, and to my ankles. I put a hand on his shoulder to balance myself as he whisks the pants away.

I feel heat rise over my neck. My grip tightens on him. This is a bad idea. I should have thought this through.

"Darlin, are you okay?"

"I...uh...I. Well, maybe." I cover my breasts with my hands, feeling exposed.

"Hey," he says as he reaches up and pulls my hands away. "Darlin, you are beautiful. You have no reason to feel shy."

"It's just. You know, three children take a toll."

"Of course they do, and it makes you all the more beautiful."

He kisses the stretch marks on each side of my abdomen, then kisses the round paunch that never seems to go away, no matter how many sit-ups I do.

"Any man who despises the look of a woman who has carried children in her body is a fool." As he stands, he pushes his pants down and off and stands with arms stretched wide. "Do I look like a man who is displeased by what he sees?"

I can't deny the evidence of his arousal standing proudly between us. The heat spreads up to my scalp, but for a different reason this time. I look away, embarrassed by my naivete.

He pulls me into his arms, his erection pressing into my stomach. With his mouth next to my ear, he whispers, "You are beautiful, Darlin. From head to toe, absolutely beautiful. You're still driving, and we still won't do anything you aren't ready for, okay?"

His words bolster my confidence, and I nod. I take his hand and lead him to the bed, where I slide in and scoot over, making room for him. He joins me and takes me in his arms, the make-out session starting anew and rekindling the heat that was put on pause by my temporary confidence crisis.

Along with kisses and embraces, our hands roam and explore. I put his hand on my breast. He fondles and squeezes, molds and teases. He kisses my neck and I cradle his head, pulling it lower.

His mouth sucks at my nipple, his teeth nipping gently and sending a sizzle of electricity through me. Each pull of his mouth is like a live wire leading directly to my clitoris. Moans of pleasure escape me.

I thought I was aroused in the kitchen, but that was a bare flickering flame compared to the inferno he's stoking in me now. His mouth returns to mine, and I kiss him, deep and hungry. In a fit of need, I grab his hand off my breast and push it down between my legs.

His fingers stroke between my lips and find me soaked. "You are needy, aren't you, Darlin?" he says against my mouth.

"Yes!" I gasp as a finger strums against my clitoris.

He kisses me, his tongue stroking in time with his finger. His thumb replaces the finger, and he presses two fingers into my slit. I move against his hand. I had no idea it could feel this good to be touched.

He pulls his mouth from mine. "Darlin, I'd like to taste you."

"What?" I think I understand what he wants, but I can't imagine that he's serious. I mean, I know people do that sort of thing, but the way Benjamin talked about it...well, it was obvious he thought it was disgusting and had convinced me I probably would, too.

Ford looks me in the eye, his hand still working between my legs. "I'd like to taste you."

"Um...okay, if you want."

The grin that spreads across his face looks like a kid who's just been handed his favorite candy. "Excellent," he says and starts kissing his way down my body.

He strokes his tongue up through the valley at my center, eliciting an "Oh my God!" from me.

That man's mouth is a miracle. Yet again, he surprises me by taking what I thought was the pinnacle of pleasurable sensations and pushing me higher.

Every lick, every suck, every flick of his tongue drives me higher and higher. My hips are moving so much he has to grip me with his hands.

I feel like I am about to lose my mind and reach down, taking his head in my hands. "Oh my God, Ford. Oh my God!"

I try to push him away, but he doesn't stop. He's on the trail of what he wants and he's not going to give up until he has it. A lash of his tongue does it and the inferno blazes out of control, wildfire burning through me from my center out, singing through my blood to consume me whole as the orgasm rides the waves of heat.

I cry out, or maybe scream out, his name as my body shudders. It's so intense, I think I might have a heart attack or maybe split into a million pieces. When I come back to myself, I'm in his arms even though I can't remember him moving.

He kisses me and I thrill at the taste of myself on his lips. It's not disgusting at all and based on the enthusiasm with which Ford applied himself to the act, he didn't find it disgusting either. I press myself against him, his erection still prominent and weeping with need.

Being with Ford has been incredible so far. There's one more hurdle to cross over and I find myself eager to experience that as well. I reach a hand between us and wrap it around his shaft.

I pull my mouth from his. "Ford."

"Yes, Darlin?"

"I want…"

"We don't have to."

"Don't you want to? I do."

He holds my eyes. "Are you sure?"

"I am," I tell him with a nod.

"I didn't bring any condoms with me, so we should wait."

"I can't get pregnant. I had my tubes tied after my daughter was born." I hadn't wanted to give Benjamin any more children. "I have also been tested a few times for STDs because I wanted to be sure nothing had been passed to me from the affairs."

He's quiet for a moment.

"I am clean. I get tested regularly at work because we're exposed to a lot of things in the course of our work."

"So, there's no reason not to, right?" I ask, smiling up at him.

In answer, he leans down and kisses me again and moves on top of me. He settles his broad body between my thighs and reaches between us, stroking the head of his cock through the swampy valley of my slit. It feels so good.

My pulse kicks up again, and I am surprised by the moaning chuckle he pulls from me. He positions himself and begins to push his way inside slowly. The pain is sharp, but not as bad as it was the first time all those years ago, probably because I know what to expect.

My body stretches to accommodate his girth. I put my hands on his shoulders, squeezing tight, my nails digging into his back. He slides out, then pushes in with a bit more force until he is buried to the hilt.

"You okay, Darlin?" he asks as he pauses, giving me time to adjust around him. He's much larger than Benjamin.

I push that thought away. Benjamin is over and done. This is Ford. I'm with Ford and it is magnificent.

I look up at Ford and nod. "Yes, I'm fine, just needed a minute."

"I know," he says and kisses me. Then he begins to move.

It's still quite tight, but my body is well lubricated, and I adjust quickly. I match his movements. After a few minutes, I bring my knees up, which pushes him even deeper.

"Gawd, Darlin..."

He picks up speed. His hips pumping hard, our bodies moving together. I didn't think it possible, but the friction between us begins to create that most lovely of pressures in my body. "Ford..." I gasp.

He is driving into me now. "Ford, I'm..."

He kisses me and lowers onto his elbows, his body covering mine. The feel of him over me is amazing. I don't feel caged, but I feel safe... protected... cherished.

I wrap my arms around him and hold on as he pounds into me over and over. The change in position creates even more friction and my already sensitive clit is sending me hurtling toward another orgasm. I know it's going to hit me fast and hard, even harder than the last one.

"Ford... Ford... Ford! I'm...Oh I'm...!" I go crashing into the abyss, my body gripping Ford's so hard that he hisses. He goes for another dozen strokes, then finds his own release with a groan, emptying himself deep inside me.

We're both breathing hard as we ride the waves of pleasure. I hold him tight as he rests his forehead against my shoulder. When the aftershocks are done, he kisses my neck and moves off me, pulling me into his arms and cuddling me there.

I finally understand what all the fuss is about.

Chapter 20

Caitlyn

Chapter 20

Caitlyn

Ford is returning to the house for breakfast, and I'm elated. When he walks through the door, he already looks worn down. I can't imagine what kind of scene he had to go to that already took that kind of toll on him.

Rather than ask him about it, I decide right then and there that I want to be his place of calm, his safe harbor. He wades through the darkest of humanity all day, every day, so I want to bring in the light.

He takes off his jacket and drapes it on the back of the chair at the dining room table, then goes to the kitchen sink to wash his hands. When he's dried them, I step into his personal space and stretch up to put a chaste kiss on his lips.

His arms go around me and pull my body against his as he deepens the kiss. I let him take what he needs and can feel him relax by degrees until his shoulders are loose beneath my hands.

"Thanks. I needed that," he says when he pulls away.

"You're welcome. It was such a hardship," I say, teasing.

He winks and gives me a gentle swat on the butt.

"I was in the mood for an omelet this morning. Is there anything you don't like? Mushrooms? Peppers? Onions?"

"Darlin, I like it all."

He watches as I pour the eggs into the saucepan, then add a generous amount of meat and vegetables, topping it off with a blend of shredded cheeses. While I work with the food, he stands behind me with his hands resting on my hips as he nuzzles my neck.

"If you keep that up," I say breathlessly, "I'm going to burn the eggs."

He chuckles, and it reverberates through my entire body. With a nip to my shoulder, he concedes. "All right. I'll behave."

"There's fresh coffee and mugs are just above it," I tell him and wave the spatula.

He pulls down a mug and fills it, then leans a hip against the counter to watch me. I fold the egg over, then slide it out onto a plate. "There is silverware on the table. Don't wait for me; eat it while it's hot. I'll be there in a minute."

"Thank you."

When I sit across from him at the table with my own breakfast, he's almost halfway through his meal. I knew he'd probably be hungry after the early morning.

"My brother is expecting me for lunch today and I was wondering if you might want to go with me," Ford says when I'm settled in my seat.

I pause to think about it. My first inclination is that I'd love to meet his brother, but when I take into consideration that this whole whatever it is between us just started a couple of days ago, I'm hesitant. Throw in the black eye and the fact that I'm still married and I hesitate more.

Rather than equivocate, I tell him my thoughts. He nods. "Yeah, I get that. I'll just call and tell them I can't make it."

I lift an eyebrow at him. "No, you won't. You need to spend time with your family."

He's clearly amused. "Snuff that fire in your eye, Darlin. It will be fine. Plus, I don't like the idea of you being here alone."

"Ford, you can't be with me twenty-four hours a day. I'll be fine. The gate will let me know if Benjamin comes through. If that happens, I'll call you."

He looks at me for a moment, then nods again. "Okay. I don't like it, but something tells me you're not going to budge."

"That would be correct."

He chuckles.

With breakfast finished and the kitchen cleaned up, we're at loose ends. I need to go through the kid's rooms, but don't want to do that while he's here. When he goes to lunch, I'll get started.

My phone rings, and my son's face fills the screen. Ford waves a hand to let me know he's going downstairs to where the television is in what used to be the kid's playroom. I nod and whisper that I'll be down soon.

"Hello love," I greet my son. "How are you and Kris?"

"We're good, Mom. I got your email. When were you thinking of coming?"

"I'm not sure, but I'm really missing seeing your faces."

"Well, as you know, we're in the new house now and we're having a housewarming soon. It would be wonderful if you could be here for that."

"Let me go to my office so I can look at my calendar."

I move quietly through the house, the drone of the television drifting up the stairs when I pass by the stairwell. The noise makes me smile. It's nice to have someone else here making noise, even if just a little.

"Okay," I say. "What's the date?"

I put the date on my calendar and assure him I'll try to make it. It would be wonderful to see them and their new home and see the friends of theirs I know again.

We talk for a while longer and I also speak to Kris for a few minutes. Those two are so well matched it makes my heart happy they found each other.

Not wanting to keep Ford waiting too long, I wrap up the call and promise I'll let them know if I'll be able to make the visit. I'd love to see them. Maybe Ford could go with me.

Thinking of Ford, I go in search of him. The television is still drifting up the stairs, so I go down. I find him with his head laid back as he quietly snores, oblivious to the television.

For a moment, I think about going upstairs and leaving him to catch up on his rest, but I sit next to him and snuggle into his side. He rouses enough to put his arm around me and pull me tight against him.

Although he stays awake a few minutes to watch the program, it doesn't take long for him to start snoring again. I smile, happy that he feels comfortable enough to relax and do what he needs.

A couple of hours later, he rouses with a snort. I'm still snuggled against his side and he leans over and kisses the top of my head.

"Sorry," he says.

"There is no need for you to be sorry. You were up in the wee hours of this morning. I'm just glad you had a chance to catch up on your sleep."

He looks at his watch. "Well, shoot."

"I know. And no, I haven't changed my mind. You need to go spend time with your family."

"All ready reading my mind, are you?"

"Maybe," I reply coyly.

Chapter 21

Ford

I hate leaving Cait alone, but she's right. She should be fine for a few hours. It was fun seeing her get all feisty with me.

When I step through the back door into the kitchen of my brother's house, I take off my jacket and hang it on the back of a chair.

"Well, I do declare," my sister-in-law, Bonnie, says, "do my eyes deceive me or is that my illusive brother?"

I lean over and kiss her cheek. "It's me. Don't get all worked up. Something smells good."

"That's me," she teases. She waves a spoon at the gun on my hip. "You could have left all that in the car."

No, I couldn't. Unless I can lock my weapon and badge away, they're on my belt. There's no way I'd ever leave them sitting unsecured in a vehicle.

"Hey," Al says, coming into the kitchen. "Glad you could make it."

I follow him into the living room where his two sons are watching mixed martial arts.

"Hiya Uncle," Robbie, Al's youngest, says in greeting.

"Hi Rob. How's school?"

"Good, but I'm ready to be done."

"Junior," I say to his other son.

"Hey," he replies.

Al returns to his recliner, and I settle into an armchair, focusing on the television. This is how it is when I come here. The menfolk watch sports on television while Bonnie fixes the meal.

Then we gather at the table and eat. The boys, both college students with busy lives, leave as soon as they've eaten. Al and I will sit in the living room while Bonnie cleans up. After a couple of hours, I leave if I haven't already been called in by work.

I love my brother and his family, and I love spending time with them, but sitting here, my mind wanders. Specifically, it wanders to Cait. I wonder what she's doing right now.

She had mentioned needing to go through the rooms her kids had used growing up, and I wish I was there to help her. Hopefully, that asshole ex-husband of hers stays away.

"Earth to Ford," Al says, breaking into my wandering thoughts.

"Huh? Sorry. What did you say?"

"I said I'm surprised you didn't get called into work this morning."

"Oh, I did. It was around four, though, so I've already been to the scene and done what I can. It will take forensics a while to go through the evidence."

"Is that what you were thinking so hard about?""Nope."

He waits for me to go on, but I don't. I understand Cait's reasons for not wanting to come with me today and honor her decision not to come. But if I let my family know about her, they're going to want to meet her as soon as possible.

It's been ages since I got divorced and I haven't brought anyone home since. Bonnie is always wanting to fix me up with someone, but I've never been agreeable. She'll be eager to meet this new woman who has turned my head.

It will have to wait until Cait's black eye heals and she feels more comfortable in our relationship. Are we in a relationship? Yeah, I believe we are. I mean, I want to be.

Although it's only been a few days, I've never felt as attracted to a woman as I am to Cait. There's never been the kind of connection I feel with her, either. She's just about perfect as far as I'm concerned.

"So, what were you thinking about?" Al persists.

I sigh. "Not a what, a who."

He raises an eyebrow at me.

"I'll tell you all about her when I'm ready."

"Her?"

"Her," I confirm.

I turn my attention back to the television, but I can feel Al's eyes on me. Surprisingly, he doesn't push the subject.

"Lunch is ready," Bonnie calls.

Like pigs being called to the trough, we get up and go to the dining room. I should have known my brother wouldn't let it go. Instead of pushing me in the living room, as we're sitting down at the table, he announces, "Ford's got a new woman."

I glare over at him.

"Oh, really," Bonnie says. "Tell me everything."

"It's new, and it's complicated," I reply.

She makes a face at me. "Complicated? Why? Is she married or something?"

I pause, then hold out my hands. "She's separated. Can we please just eat this amazing smelling food before I get called back out?"

"Fine, but you're going to tell me everything," she concedes, putting one hand in mine and her other in her husband's.

Everyone joins hands around the table, and we bow our heads as Al says grace. A heartbeat after he says "Amen" and it's echoed around the table, Bonnie dives back in.

"You can talk and eat at the same time," she says, looking at me pointedly.

"She's forty-five. We met at the gym. She's been separated for some time."

"For some time?" she echoes, making a question of it.

"Yes," I confirm. "It's complicated and none of your business at this point."

She harrumphs, but lets it go finally.

Toward the end of the meal, Bonnie says, "You should bring her with you next weekend if you're not working."

I nod. "She may be going to Denver to see one of her sons, but if she's back and I'm not working, I'll ask her."

"We have a game on Saturday morning," Al says. "We're playing the Wildcats across town at their field."

From there, we talk about football and new plays he's wanting to try with the kids. This is a topic I can engage in whole-heartedly. We talk strategy and play structure for a while.

I'm not sure eight-year-olds warrant as much time and energy as Al puts into working out complicated plays, but he enjoys it, so I go along. Mostly, the kids all just run after the ball and hopefully make it across the goal line occasionally. The correct goal line, that is.

Al doesn't get too uptight but mostly wants them to have fun, and that makes him a brilliant coach for this age group. The kids all think he's pretty great and know when he's serious, it's time to pay attention.

My nephews finish eating in record time despite their mom peppering them with questions about school. Al Junior is a senior at Oklahoma State and Robbie is a sophomore. Neither Al nor Betty graduated from college and they are doing everything they can to make sure their boys do.

The boys take off and I stay a while longer, but the urge to get back to Cait is strong. That should probably concern me, but it doesn't.

Chapter 22

Caitlyn

I decide to go ahead and meet my friends for lunch on Tuesday. There was some hesitancy because the evidence of Benjamin's elbow to my eye is still prominent and turning that lovely sickly yellow-green of healing injuries. Arnica cream has helped, but not enough.

I apply enough makeup to cover it for the most part, but anyone who knows me as well as my gal pals will be able to see right through it. Before I enter the restaurant, I take a deep breath and stand up straight. I'll do my best to help them focus on the good that's happening in my life instead of the one bit of bad that will soon be rooted firmly in the past.

Monica and Sheryl are already seated at our table. "Hello ladies," I say, taking my usual seat.

Monica scrutinizes me. After a moment, she says, "Your hair looks wonderful, Cait. I also like the new outfit."

"Thank you," I say, my hand going to my hair.

Sheryl holds out an envelope to me. "Your appraisal came in. I think you'll be pleased."

"Excellent," I reply, taking the envelope. "I was hoping you'd have it for me."

It ends up just being the three of us. Francine had children later in life and one of her poor girls is down with the flu. I miss seeing her but am happy for her to keep the germs at home. That is one thing I don't miss about having little ones, the revolving door of illnesses that follow children home from school regularly.

We're about halfway through lunch when Monica finally asks, "So, are we just supposed to ignore that splotch of extra heavy makeup around your eye?"

I sigh. "I would like that, yes."

She just raises an eyebrow at me while Sheryl looks between us. Sheryl is a bit of a Pollyanna who likes to keep her rose-colored glasses firmly in place. She doesn't do well with conflict.

However, I don't begrudge her worldview. I wish more people could focus on all the sweet and positive things in the world. It's probably what makes her such a good realtor. People feel good when they're with her.

"I cut Ben off. Financially, that is. He was expecting his usual extra bit of allowance I've been giving him and didn't get it. He got mad, came by the house and made threats. Then we got into a tussle over my purse because he thought...well, I guess he thought I'd have a wad of cash in it, which just goes to show how little he actually knows about me. He accidentally elbowed me in the eye."

"Did you call the police?" Sheryl asks with concern.

"I did not. It really was an accident," I reply. "But one of the guards had followed Ben to the house because of the way he was acting and saw what happened. The guard called the police."

"Aren't you concerned about the threats?" Monica asks.

"Not anymore."

They both look at me askance. They won't let it go. I'll have to tell them.

"There is this man I met at the gym, and we've become some-what...friendly. Just casual conversations and chit chat. He is a homicide detective with the OKCPD. He found out about the struggle with Ben and the black eye, and he insisted on staying over."

Sheryl gasps.

"In the downstairs bedroom," I clarify. "Ben returned the next night, as he said he would. Ford, my friend, was there. He was in the bathroom when Ben came in. Ben was ranting and raving and was making threats when Ford came in and put his gun to the back of Ben's head."

Monica whoops. "I'll bet that got his attention."

Sheryl claps.

"It did," I confirmed. "Ben is still angry, but he will think twice before coming back to the house."

"Can't you lock him out?" Monica asks.

I tell her about being legally unable to shut him out of the house and Sheryl confirms it. "As long as it's his home, too, she can't lock him out."

I hold up the envelope Sheryl gave me. "But with this, I am going to make him an offer I hope he won't be able to refuse. In exchange for half the proceeds from the house, I'm going to ask him to sign an agreement that my attorney is drawing up that requires him to give up his access to the house. Then I'll be able to lock him out."

"You shouldn't have to do that," Monica says, "but I understand that it's a straightforward route to get free of him."

Sheryl adds, "Since you can afford it, tell him you'll pay it out now rather than waiting for the house to sell if he'll file for divorce." They both know the details of the prenup we signed.

I hadn't thought of that, but it's a good idea. Now that he's been cut off from receiving additional proceeds, there's no reason for him to stay married to me. Even if I were to die, he wouldn't get anything from it, regardless of whether we were married.

"So, who is this detective we've heard absolutely nothing about?" Monica asks.

I sigh. I had hoped that when we skipped past that to the issue with Ben, they would forget about me mentioning Ford. That had been wishful thinking, apparently. I tell them all about the man with whom I've become so enamored.

We finish our lunch, and I call Ms. Hartmann from the car. She has the contract ready but was waiting for me to provide her with the appraisal amount. I tell her about Sheryl's idea, and she agrees it might be a splendid avenue to follow. If Benjamin divorces me, it will negate the need to invalidate the prenuptial agreement.

It would definitely be an easier resolution. It can't hurt to ask, right? She promises me she'll have the contract updated and sent to me by end of day.

Once I have the contract in hand, I'll need to set a time to meet with Benjamin. I'd feel safest if I could set it at a time when Ford can come, too, but he is in the middle of investigating the murders he was called to early Sunday morning. We've been in contact every day, but I haven't seen him since he left to have lunch with his brother's family.

Maybe I should leave Ford out of it. He has a very demanding, stressful job and I'm sure the last thing he needs is me using him as a crutch. I've been independent for the better part of two decades, so having a meeting with my husband should be no big deal.

Sure, no big deal. I'm feeling braver, but his unpredictable nature spurs me to be smart, so I call Monica. Benjamin has always been a little afraid of her. If Ford can come, that will be great, but just in case he can't, I want to hedge my bets and have a backup available.

Monica is the best backup I know.

Chapter 23

Caitlyn

"Do you think he'll come alone?" Monica asks as she sips her wine.

"I'm not sure," I tell her, putting the tray of finger foods I've prepared on the counter. "I guess he might bring his mistress, or maybe an attorney. There's just no telling with him. I hope it's just him, though."

"Yeah, less drama," she agrees. She takes the tray into the dining room and puts it on the table. I don't know that anyone will want to eat, but the hostess in me can't help but have something available.

I have invited Benjamin to the house to discuss the sale of the property. When I called him, he wanted to meet right away. Although I'm happy to get it out of the way, that means Ford is less likely to be here.

I called Ford and told him what was going on, but he's being run ragged with his current case. I assured him he didn't need to come, but he said he'd be here if he could. I don't think Benjamin will act out with Monica here; at least, I hope he won't.

But then I never would have thought he'd do the things he's done the last two times I've seen him.

Besides the original document she prepared for me, the attorney also provided a document to be given to Benjamin to let him know a timeframe for removing his property prior to the sale. She suggested I have a witness present to verify that the document is given to him and that he's told what it is. Hence, Monica's presence has the dual purpose of backup and witness.

I check the clock on the wall. There are about ten minutes to go before the appointment time we set. I think about going upstairs to powder my nose but decide I don't care how I look. I don't even care that I have on no makeup, which leaves the fading bruise around my eye easily seen.

"Honey, I'm home!" Ben calls from the front door.

My lip curls in distaste. I look at Monica to see her rolling her eyes and I bust out with a laugh. She grins back at me.

"Are you that happy to see me?" Ben asks as he enters the kitchen, mistaking our laughter. He waltzes over to the refrigerator like he still lives here and pulls out a beer.

I catch motion out of the corner of my eye near the door and look over to see a very young, very pregnant woman. Benjamin makes no effort to introduce her, but I recognize her from Boston.

"Hi, I'm Monica, Cait's friend. Can I get you something to drink?" Monica asks the girl. That's what Ben's mistress looks like, barely more than a girl.

"Hi, I'm Heather," the girl replies shyly. "I don't need anything to drink, but thank you. At this stage, if I drink much of anything, I have to go to the bathroom five minutes later."

Benjamin strolls out of the kitchen and into the dining room and slouches into the seat at the head of the table. I want to make a rude comment about that not being his seat any longer, but decide not to stir up unnecessary problems. Heather follows him like a puppy toddling along at his heels.

"Oh my goodness, she looks like you at nineteen, but without the backbone," Monica whispers to me. "She sounds like she's only about twelve, though."

"Let's get this over with," I whisper back, taking my glass of wine in one hand and her hand in my other as we go into the other room. We're just about to sit when someone knocks on the door.

"I'll get it," Monica says.

I hear low voices as she answers the door. It's definitely a man, but that's all I can tell. She comes back into the room with a smirk of a smile on her face. Ford walks through the door behind her.

My heart leaps at the sight of him, but then I take in everything about him and see how exhausted he looks. My excitement is replaced with concern. He rounds the table to me, then leans down and kisses me as he cups my head in one of his large hands.

"Hey Darlin," he says. He takes off his jacket and hangs it on the back of a chair, which leaves his badge and holstered gun on full display.

Monica watches Ford and raises an eyebrow at me.

"Sit down, honey. You look tired," I tell him.

"I am," he replies.

"Do you want something to drink?" I ask.

"I'll take one of those beers I like, but stay put, I'll get it," he says.

I smile inwardly at the blatant way Ford is clarifying that he's been in my home for more than just a casual visit. He's staking his claim in the way that men do and throwing it in Benjamin's face.

"Can we get this show on the road already?" Benjamin complains.

I narrow my eyes at him to see him glaring at Ford's back as it disappears through the kitchen door.

"Certainly," I say, and pull over the envelope of papers I had placed on the table earlier. I find the notification document and take it out first. I hand it to him and say the words the attorney said it was important to speak.

"This is an official notification of my intent to sell the house and informing you that you have fourteen days from today's date, expiring at midnight two Wednesdays from today, to remove any belongings you wish to keep out of those items in your room."

I give him a moment for that to sink in.

"Anything not in your room has been purchased by the estate and is not available for you to remove from the property. Therefore, you will only be allowed to remove your items with supervision by the trustee of the estate."

I pause again, wanting to take my time to be sure he hears everything.

"If you choose not to remove your items within the fourteen days allowed, any remaining items will be disposed of at the discretion of the trustee. You are not required to sign or acknowledge this document in any way, but the service of this document is being witnessed by all parties present."

Ford returns and sits in the chair next to mine as he says, "So witnessed." He opens his beer and takes a long pull.

Benjamin picks up the first document, glances at it and sets it aside.

I take out the next document, but I don't hand it to Benjamin yet.

"Now, for the main reason I asked you here. I understand you are upset at the thought of me selling the house, even though you no longer live here. I have explained to you that the house did not belong to us but belongs to the trust and therefore, you are not legally owed any proceeds from the sale. However, I have come up with a proposal that I would like to present to you."

I take a deep breath. This is the part that I most want him to accept.

"If you will file for an uncontested divorce, upon it being finalized, I will pay you half of the appraised value of the house, which at today's market value, half would be just under two million dollars."

I hand the document to him.

"The proposal is spelled out in this document, and you will see the official appraisal as an attached exhibit. If you choose not to proceed with the divorce, you will receive exactly what you are legally entitled to when the house sells, which, as I said, is nothing."

Ben flips through the pages to the appraisal in the back. He's got his poker face on and isn't letting any reaction show. "Why would I want to divorce you?" he asks and hooks a thumb at Ford. "Are you trying to free yourself up for him?"

"Why would you not divorce me?" I ask and go on, ignoring his second question. "You have a child on the way with Heather, don't you want to marry her? Even if you don't, there is no benefit to you staying married to me."

Maybe he thinks I was kidding when I said I wouldn't give him an allowance anymore.

"There's no more allowance. If I die, you get nothing whether we're married or not. I changed my will to cut you out a long time ago. The children are provided for in amounts that ensure that they would never have to work again if they didn't want to, but the largest portion of the trust goes to charity."

Ben's face turns red with anger. I hold his gaze. I start to look away as it grows uncomfortable, but Ford puts his hand on my thigh, and I stay strong. Ben looks away first.

I go on. "The proposal has the same fourteen-day expiration date as the first document. A lack of response will be construed as a refusal of the proposal."

Ben lunges up out of his chair, causing the table to rattle. "Let's go," he barks at Heather, who flinches in response.

Ford's hand tightens on my thigh. The three of us remain at the table as we listen to Ben stomping through the house. His exit is punctuated by the slamming of the front door.

I let out my breath.

"That was brilliant!" Monica says.

"Well done, Darlin," Ford says as he pulls over the tray of food and starts eating.

"I can fix you something more substantial to eat," I tell him.

"This will do fine."

"So. You're the mystery man," Monica says to Ford, who looks up at her.

"I guess I am," Ford replies after he swallows down one of the tiny finger sandwiches.

"She's fantastic, you know, and she deserves someone who recognizes that, especially after being with an asshole like Benjamin."

"I know, and I agree," he says, looking Monica in the eye. "I can't say I'm the best man for her, but I think she's fantastic, too, and intend to remind her of it every chance I get."

Monica watches him for a long moment. I'm not sure what she sees in his eyes, but she nods. "I'm going to get gone and leave you two alone."

"Mon, you don't have to..." I start.

"Yes, I do. You haven't seen each other for a few days, and he looks like he's ready to drop, so I'm sure he'd like a few moments alone with you before he does."

"I appreciate that," Ford says. "It was nice to meet you, Monica."

Monica goes into the kitchen and gathers her things. I walk with her to the door. "He's handsome in a rough and tumble kind of way," she says low.

My lips tilt up on one side. "I know."

"I like him."

"Me, too."

"Is he good in bed?" she asks seriously.

"Monica!" I hiss out at her, but I can't help grinning. I bite my lower lip and nod.

"Hallelujah! It's about time. I'm ecstatic for you, Cait. You deserve some happiness in your life." She hugs me. "Call me if you need anything," she says and goes out the front door to her car.

"I will," I call after her. "You do the same."

She lifts a hand in a wave before getting into her car and driving away.

Chapter 24

Caitlyn

I return to the dining room to find Ford has eaten almost everything on the tray. I stop behind him and knead his tense looking shoulders. "You didn't have to come tonight. I know you're busy with work, but I'm glad you were here."

He groans. "I wanted to see you and I'm glad I was here, too. That guy's an asshole."

I laugh. "Yes, he is. You're so tight," I say, my fingers barely able to work his muscles. "We can go get in the hot tub if you want."

"That sounds like heaven, but I didn't bring a suit."

I kiss the top of his head. "It is just you and I here. We don't need suits."

"Perfect. Let's go skinny dipping, but no funny business. I might pass out and drown from the exertion."

I laugh again. "No funny business, I promise," I say as I go to the panel on the wall to turn the lights on at the tub. I thought he might need to relax if he could make it and had started the tub warming a few hours ago in anticipation. It was easy enough to shut it back down if he didn't come.

He stands and faces me. I take his tie in my hand and undo it. With quick fingers, I unbutton his shirt as he removes his holster and badge and sets them on the table. I take them and put them in a drawer in the buffet at the side of the room so they're not sitting out in the open.

Although I seriously doubt anyone will come into the house, with Ben being so angry when he left and having a key to all the doors, I'd rather be safe by putting it away. When I return to Ford, his shirt and shoes are off and he's working on his belt. I push his hands out of the way and take over. It's nice to have someone to take care of again.

Once he's down to his stocking feet, I grab the hem of the jersey dress I'm wearing and pull it off over my head. When it's off, I see Ford staring at my underwear.

"There is a lingerie store near where I have lunch with Monica and a couple of other friends on Tuesdays. I stopped in after lunch yesterday and picked this up. Do you like it?"

"Darlin, that is doing nothing to help me relax."

"Well, let me get rid of it then," I say and proceed to take it off, which makes Ford suck in a breath.

I take him by the hand and lead him onto the back patio. The tile is cool underfoot, so we hurry to the hot water. Ford steps in as I grab a couple of towels from the storage cabinet nearby and place them close to the tub for when we get out.

He reaches out a hand to me as I step in. The hot water feels wonderful, and I realize I was a little stressed out by this evening's events and needed to relax, too. Ford wraps an arm around my waist and pulls me onto his lap.

"I've missed you," he says.

I put my forehead to his. "I've missed you, too."

We sit there for a long time, him letting the jets work on his back and me just enjoying being with him.

"Do you think Ben will take the offer?" he asks, breaking the silence.

"I think he'd be foolish not to, but I have no idea what goes on in that man's head. He has never made sense to me."

"Enough about him. How are you doing with all of this?"

I shrug. "I'm okay. I'm just ready for it to be over with. It feels like I've been living in a holding pattern for over twenty years. When Maggie told me she wouldn't be coming back to Oklahoma, something clicked and let me know it was time. Time to move on. Time to be free and get on with my life."

"That's understandable," he says as he starts kissing my neck.

I tilt my head to give him better access.

"Oh, that's nice," I say. His hand slides up my thigh, making me giggle. "I thought you said no funny business!"

"You changed my mind," he says, adding nibbles between his kisses.

"I didn't do anything."

"Darlin', you are all kinds of temptation, without even trying. I just look at you and my mind conjures a dozen ways I want to make love to you." He nips at my shoulder.

"Oh...my," I say, a little breathless.

Moving slowly, I adjust my position on his lap so that I'm facing him, straddling him. We make love in the hot tub, slow and steady, tender, and unhurried. I can't seem to get enough of him, and I am enjoying every minute. The enjoyment of sex is such a surprising and welcome sensation.

Once we're snuggled together in bed, I think about how much my life has changed in such a short time. I should probably be frightened, but I'm not. Although I don't know everything about Ford, I know he is worthy of my trust.

He has given me no evidence that he would ever lie and cheat. He seems to only want me and, by all appearances, doesn't care about my money.

I have no doubt that when or if he tires of me, he will tell me. If that happens, we'll go our separate ways. That thought makes me a little sad, but I remind myself that my track record with men is less than stellar and my judgment regarding romance isn't very trustworthy.

Ford and I are having fun and I shouldn't read too much into it no matter how much I want to. My nature is to try to plan the future, but for the first time in my life, I will not plan, nor am I going to float along anymore.

I'm going to be an active participant in my life and focus on what brings me joy. Ford brings me joy, and that's all that matters for now.

Chapter 25

Caitlyn

I'm just about to order dinner when Gabriella sits down at my table. To give her time to settle in, I ask the server to give us a few moments.

I was almost positive I would be eating dinner alone at the Society. Although I have a million things to do and I started not to come myself, since it was my idea for our group to meet for dinner on Thursdays, I came.

A workout before would have been wonderful, but I wasn't about to wear a bunch of makeup while exercising and I didn't want to go around flashing my still bruised face. Instead, I applied a liberal amount of concealer and makeup and just came for dinner.

I thought that if I didn't bother to show up, my credibility with the other women would take a hit, and that's not the way I want to start. My professing the accidental nature of the injury would probably be suspect, too.

"Hi Gabriella! It's so good to see you again," I say in greeting.

"Hello Cait! It's good to be seen," she says, grinning at me. "It's good to see you, too. How has your week been?"

"Good. I've put my house on the market recently, so it's been a busy few days getting it ready for showings and all that fun stuff."

"Ugh!" she says. "That is a lot of work. People don't realize what it takes. I've seen it with my clients and it's enough to make me want to never move again."

I love that the conversation is coming easily. It's my hope that these women become good friends, but I especially felt a connection with Gabriella.

"If I didn't dislike the place so much, I'd be tempted to stay put, too."

"Oh? Why do you dislike it?"

"It was a gift from my father. It was more his style than mine, but now that the kids are grown, I'm ready to downsize."

"So it's just you and your husband?"

For a moment, I hesitate at the question, unsure how to respond without getting into the whole drawn out saga. I decide to keep it simple.

"No," I reply. "Really, it's just me. I'm in process of a divorce." I hope.

"I'm sorry to hear that."

"Don't be," I assure her. "It really is a good thing and has been a long time coming."

"Do you have an area of the City you want to move to?"

That starts a discussion about the various neighborhoods around town, their merits and concerns. She turns out to be a great resource. Gabriella has done a bit of work all over town and is well versed on the metro as a whole.

A woman comes to our table. "I'm so sorry to interrupt," she says. "You're Gabriella Carmichael, right?"

"Yes, I am," Gabriella answers.

"My name is Mitzi Parrish. My husband and I are thinking about remodeling our house. I was wondering if you had a card so that I might contact you and set up an appointment."

"Certainly," Gabriella says. She picks up her purse and pulls out a card, handing it to the woman. "Call or email me and we'll set something up."

"I will," Mitzi says. "I'll let you get back to your meal."

Gabriella maintains her professional demeanor until the woman is across the room. Then she looks at me, grinning. "That's the third time someone has asked for my card just this week! I was unsure about paying so much money to join this place, but it looks like I'm going to cover that cost quickly if these inquiries pan out."

"That's fantastic!" I reply, truly happy for her.

"I was a little hesitant. I mean, the business will be great, but I mostly wanted the connections and I'm so socially awkward that I thought it would be a disaster."

Her comment surprises me. "What? You don't seem awkward at all."

"I'm good one on one, but groups make me nervous. My background is probably very different from a lot of these women's backgrounds, and a childhood of poverty doesn't make for learning all the proper social niceties."

"Don't ever think because someone grew up differently from you that you are in any way less than they are," I say, putting my hand on hers.

I've seen this kind of doubt in women before. Why is it we always seem to think we're on the verge of being found out as imposters?

"Thank you. My heart knows that, but my head gets in the way of it sometimes."

The server returns to take our orders. I know what I want, but Gabriella and I have been talking, and she hasn't had a chance to review the menu. "Go ahead," she says. "It won't take me but a second to decide."

Sure enough, once I tell the server what I want, she has already decided what she wants. When he departs with our orders in hand, we return to talking.

"So, are you married? Do you have any children?" I ask to maneuver the conversation onto lighter ground.

"No. Not married, no children."

"Do you have a boyfriend?"

"No," she says, shaking her head. "I just started my business a few years ago, and it's been a lot of work to get it off the ground. There just hasn't been time for a serious relationship."

"That's understandable," I agree.

Elizabeth Kaizen stops by our table next. She was the one to welcome our group of newcomers to the Society. "Hello ladies," she says. "It's good to see you again. I hope you're enjoying your evening."

"We are," I assure her.

Gabriella smiles and nods in agreement.

"I won't take much of your time. I'm one of the organizers of the annual Masquerade Gala at the Skirvin. As you probably know, it's a fundraiser for Allied Arts and one of the main avenues for donations is through a silent auction. I'm reaching out to the women of the Society to ask that you consider donating an item to the auction."

"What kinds of donations do you prefer?" Gabriella asks.

"It can be pretty much anything," Elizabeth replies. "In the past, we've received art, getaways, or often, services. Anything you can donate would be greatly appreciated and, of course, since it's for charity, it would provide you with a tax benefit."

All those wrapped up items in storage come to mind. There are a few things I was on the fence about and put into storage, but they would probably do well as donations.

"I'm in process of downsizing," I tell her. "I may have a piece of art or two that might be good."

"That would be fantastic, Cait. Just let me know and I'll get with you about how to arrange for pickup."

"I'll do that."

"Anyway, I'll let you get back to your dinner. Have a wonderful evening, ladies," Elizabeth says with a small wave of her hand as she turns toward the next table to solicit donations.

"This place is going to take some getting used to," Gabriella says.

"Don't feel pressured to give if you don't want to," I tell her. "Fundraisers will always make is seem as if the organization will crumble without your donation, but rest assured, in the vast majority of cases, it will not. I learned that lesson early on when I took over my family's trust. I focus on giving to those I hold closest to my heart that address concerns about which I feel most strongly, mostly related to women's issues."

"You said you've been on the board for nonprofits. Which ones, if you don't mind me asking?"

"Oh, I don't mind," I answer. "I sat on a few boards many years ago, but for the last several years, I've been involved with the Women's Coalition. That's where I met Demi's former fiancé."

"I'm an artist, so I like the idea of donating to an arts organization," Gabriella says.

"Allied Arts is a wonderful organization with a solid reputation. I always like to check out how much of their funds go to administrative costs versus the end goal. If an organization is collecting donations just to have the majority go to their staff, that's not a group I'll donate to. Now, where were we? Ah yes, your busyness with business. What inspired you to set out on your own?"

She smiles to herself. "A few years ago, I was working for a man doing essentially what I do now. He hired me for my artistic abilities while I was still in college. I had talent, but he taught me everything I know when it comes to applying my art to the job. I worked for him for years until it became a less than desirable situation."

She takes a drink of water and I notice that her shoulders have risen with tension. "We were involved in more ways than just work. One day, a stranger asked me why I was still working for my boss. He knew my boss' less than stellar reputation. The short, neat version is that I quit, went out on my own, worked my tail off, and the rest is history."

It would appear that Gabriella and I have some commonalities beyond just being members of the Society. I like her and I think we're going to be great friends.

"I'm proud of you," I tell her. "It takes a lot of moxie to make that kind of leap. Did you ever see the stranger again to thank him?"

She shakes her head. "I've thought about seeking him out a time or two, but no. He was very...intense...and more than a bit intimidating. His family owns a very large, very successful construction company."

"Would that be Masters Construction?" I ask. "I know Beckett Masters. He's also on the board for the Coalition. He's not the intimidating type, though. He and his two brothers run the company, though, so maybe it was one of them."

"It was Masters Construction, and Morgan is the one I met."

"It seems as if fate had a reason for him to cross your path that day. Perhaps it will connect you both again someday."

She shrugs. "Perhaps."

The rest of our meal continues uninterrupted. We say our goodbyes in the dining room as we are headed in different directions, Gabriella to the fitness center and me to the lobby.

As I'm headed out, the fortune teller machine catches my eye where it squats in the lounge's corner. I smile to myself as I think how silly it was to make that wish. It looks like the entire issue will be resolved with no such violent measures.

My phone rings just as I get into my car. As if the merest thought of him conjured him, the caller ID says Benjamin. I accept the call and say, "Hello."

"Why haven't you returned my calls?"

"I haven't had any calls from you until this one," I reply.

"I've left you messages at the house."

My inclination is to get testy with him. Who does he think he is to be demanding of my time or require immediate responses? However, I take a calming breath and speak civilly. I need him to be agreeable enough to take the deal I've offered.

"Well, I'm not at the house, so I haven't gotten your messages."

"Where are you?"

"That's none of your business. What do you want, Benjamin?"

"I want to know why you're trying to screw me over?"

"How exactly am I doing that?" I ask.

"You're trying to cheat me out of what I'm owed."

"Actually, I'm offering to give you significantly more than you're legally owed." I correct him.

"You stop paying my allowance and now you're trying to kick me out of my own home..."

I interrupt him. My pleasant mood after good food and delightful conversation is quickly souring. He's trying to pick a fight and I will not be baited.

"You never cared about that house any more than you ever cared about me. It was a status symbol to you, and I was never anything more than a potential payday. You've gotten paid in the form of an allowance that you were never owed, and I don't feel the need to give you pity payments any longer. You have the documents and the only way you're going to see any further money from me or the trust is if you go through with the uncontested divorce."

Okay, so maybe I took the bait a little, but I'm sick of his bullying.

"Divorce me or don't," I say. "Frankly, I don't care anymore. I just want to be rid of you. Other than our children, you've never given me anything but heartache and headaches. I consider myself lucky that there wasn't an STD in the mix as well."

I hear him suck in a breath. Yes, it was harsh, but I really don't care anymore. It is the truth, and he needs to know I will not let him push me around any longer.

"Give me the money and I'll file for divorce," he says.

"You've lied to me too many times for me to trust you to ever be truthful or follow through on a promise. You've got the paperwork. You get the divorce and I'll cut you a check for half the value of the house the moment the divorce is final. From what I've seen, an uncontested divorce can be finalized in less than two weeks."

"What happened to you, Cait? You've become such a bitch."

"You happened to me, Benjamin. I'm just giving it back to you the same way you've given it to me since we married. My new attorney is sharp, and she believes she has a way to break the prenup. If you don't divorce me, you get zero dollars from me or from the trust. Zero. I don't know why you can't seem to grasp that concept."

"Did that nigger cop put you up to this?" He spits.

It's my turn to suck in a breath. "How dare you use that word? Ford is something you will never be, Benjamin, a decent and honorable man. You are a reprehensible, spineless, boil on the backside of humanity and aren't worthy of breathing the same air as a man like Ford. You know what? Don't sign the paperwork. I kind of like the idea of you being left with nothing."

Pulse pounding in my ears, I disconnect the call. I cannot wait for the next two weeks to be over.

One way or another, the waiting game will be over, and I'll have a path to move forward. Either Benjamin will file for divorce, or I will tell Andrea to move forward with breaking the prenup.

My phone rings again. I start to ignore it, thinking it's likely Benjamin calling me back, but I check the readout to see Ford's name.

"Hi there," I say, answering the phone with a smile.

"Hey Darlin. You at home?"

"No, I just finished dinner with a friend, but I am headed toward home. I'm in midtown now."

"Care for some company?"

"I'm always happy to have your company, Ford."

It's true, too. He makes me happy and knowing he's there for me helps me calm down.

"I'm going to go home to shower, change, grab something to eat and I'll meet you at your place."

"I made some enchiladas for lunch. There's plenty left over if you don't want to cook."

"Darlin, that sounds perfect. I'll see you in a bit."

"Okay, see you soon," I agree and disconnect.

Just like that, with a few words from Ford, my bad mood fades away.

Chapter 26

Ford

I can't seem to stay away from Cait. I keep trying to give her space, to ease her into a relationship or whatever this is between us. However, every time I resolve not to call her, to give her a night off from me, I find myself dialing her number. I'll have the idea to just talk for a minute and say good night, but my mouth has a mind of its own once she answers.

She says she's always happy to have my company, but I don't know if that's just her saying what she thinks I want to hear or whether it's really true. I hope it's true, but I have no idea if she's feeling the same way I'm starting to feel and I don't want to push her. For Christ's sake, the woman is still married.

The only time we've spent apart over the past few weeks is when my work has kept me away. I hope she doesn't think that it's all about me and that we're only together when it's convenient for me. I also hope she doesn't think it's just about sex.

In these past couple of weeks with her, I've had more sex than I've had in the last few years, and it's been fantastic. It's not just the frequency, it's because it is with her and it's not the only reason I want to see her. She's filled that Cait shaped hole in my life and I don't know what I'll do if she ever doesn't want to fill it any longer.

"Hi Ford!" She says, opening her front door to me. She puts her arm around my waist and stretches up to kiss me.

"Hey Darlin," I reply, kissing her back.

She leads me on the familiar path through the house to the kitchen. A realization hits me. Since we've been spending time together, it's always been me coming to her house, her feeding me, and we sleep together most of the time after having sex. That's not right.

"Darlin," I say. "Do you like the blues?"

She turns to look at me with her head cocked and an ornery grin on her face. "The music, the color, or the emotion?"

That makes me laugh. "The music."

"Yes, I do."

"Good. I would like to take you on a date to hear some good music."

"I like the sound of that," she says. "When are we going?"

"Next weekend, Saturday night, if you're available. My nephew plays with a great blues band and they have a gig in Tulsa."

"I am available and I'm all yours."

She sets a plate of enchiladas in front of me and they smell amazing. Everything she puts in front of me is amazing.

"Have you ever thought about being a chef?" I ask.

She laughs. "No. I'm good with family meals and comfort food, but I'm far from a chef."

"Well, you're a ten-star chef as far as I'm concerned," I say, digging into the food. "What did you get up to today?"

That gets another laugh out of her, then she tells me about her day and the dinner tonight at the society. I think it's good for her to get out and make some new friends. She's spent too much time cloistered in this big old ugly house, even if it was in the name of home and family.

"What time is your flight tomorrow?" I ask.

"I leave at nine. The flight is almost two hours, but because of the time difference, I arrive at a little before ten, Denver time. Hopefully, traffic won't be as bad after the bulk of rush hour is over."

"Are they going to pick you up?"

"No. I have a rental car reserved. They'll both be working, but Kris works from home, so he'll be there to let me in when I get to their house."

She's excited to go visit her son and his husband for their housewarming. It bothers her that all her children live so far away, but I think it hurts her most that her oldest won't speak to her. I can't imagine what someone like Cait could have done to warrant that kind of reaction.

She says he's a lot like his father. I get that, but she's his mom. My mother is long gone, and I'd do almost anything to have her back for even one day. Maybe someday he'll get his head on straight and realize what he's missing out on. For her sake, I hope so.

"When are you flying home?"

"Sunday afternoon."

When she tries to take my empty plate away, I pull her onto my lap and nuzzle her neck. She giggles at first, but when my lips graze her neck, she goes soft and wraps her arms around me.

"Mmm..." she half moans, half hums.

It's on the tip of my tongue to ask - What am I going to do without you for two and a half days? I don't though. That wouldn't be fair to her and I don't want her to feel like she needs to be here waiting around for me to have time for her.

"Can you stay over?" she asks.

"Yes, honey, I can."

"Good. I'll take all of you I can get."

She stands and takes my plate, rinses it and puts it into the dishwasher. Her calm acceptance of the realities of my life is a relief. However, I never want to take advantage of her. I hope she means what she said, but I feel compelled to make sure.

"Hey," I say. "Are you good with this? I mean, I don't want you to feel like everything has to be on my terms."

From across the room, she looks at me and cocks her head, her brow furrowed.

"I don't feel that way. You have a demanding job. I understand that, and the City is safer with you doing what you do. Besides, I'm not some dewy-eyed girl that needs someone to complete her or constantly build up her self-esteem. I meant it when I said I'll take all of you I can get."

"All right then," I say. "Promise me you'll talk to me if you start to feel differently."

She comes back to sit on my lap, and I gather her in my arms. "I promise I will. Now, why don't you take me upstairs and..."

With her lips close to my ear and her warm breath caressing over my skin, she tells me all the carnal things she wants me to do to her. My dick starts to harden, fully on board with her ideas.

"Yes, ma'am," I say and take her by the hand to lead her upstairs to her bedroom. You have got to love a classy lady with a dirty mind.

Chapter 27

Caitlyn

Ford and I leave at the same time the next morning after he kisses me thoroughly and asks me to stay in contact while I'm gone. When I considered this trip, I hesitated, wondering if Benjamin might do something while I was gone.

However, since Ford and I already moved the most valuable items into storage, the only things left for him to damage were my cherished gifts from Monica. I doubted he would do anything to them, though, because it would piss Monica off and Benjamin had always been a little afraid of her. It was a mystery to me as to why, but he was.

I put Benjamin out of my mind. If he's going to do something, he's probably going to do it whether I'm there, or not. Sheryl's supposed to have an open house on Sunday before I get home, and she'll let me know if anything is amiss. Now is the time to focus on this weekend and loving on my son and son-in-law.

Their new house is farther from the airport than their old one, but it's closer to Tommy's office. It's also larger. I can't imagine what they paid for it because real estate is so expensive in this area. Thankfully, they both have jobs that pay them well.

An idea comes to mind. Once the divorce comes through from Benjamin and I give him a check for half the value of the house, maybe I could go ahead and give some money to the children as well.

There is more in the trust than I could ever spend in my lifetime, so why not give the kids some financial help when they most need it? They're all getting established in their lives and could use it to pay off or purchase homes or use it in some other way that would enrich their lives.

Kris answers the door when I ring the bell. He's a tall, burly man with a barrel chest. His dark hair and beard are perfectly coifed and even though he's working from home, he is dressed to impress in charcoal slacks and a plum colored shirt that makes the green in his hazel eyes stand out.

"Mom!" he says and pulls me into a hug. "Welcome to our new home."

"Hello honey," I say, and tilt my head so he can kiss me on the cheek.

Holding out a hand, he ushers me inside and takes my suitcase. Once I've shrugged out of my coat, he takes it from me and hangs it in the closet in the entry. "How was your flight?" he asks.

"It was fine. It was so quick, it was a breeze. I think I spent more time waiting to board and finding my way to the car rental afterward than I actually spent on the flight."

"That's the way of it these days. Come on, I'll show you to your room, but I've been forbidden from showing you anything else other than the kitchen. Tom wants to do the grand tour with you, but he wants you to make your hummus. He says he never gets it right."

That makes me smile. Tommy always did love my hummus. Kris leads me upstairs to a guest bedroom, where he places my suitcase on the bed.

"I'll change into something I can cook in and will be down in a few minutes."

"Take your time, Mom. I'll be in the office downstairs across the hall from the kitchen if you need me."

"Thank you, son."

He leaves me alone in the room and I unpack. Once everything is hung and my toiletries are placed in the en suite bathroom, I change into something comfortable and go back downstairs to the kitchen.

Tommy breezes through the door several hours later and sweeps me up into a hug. "Mom! I'm so glad you're here!"

"Hello, honey," I say, laughing as he turns us in a circle.

Tommy takes after me more than my other two children. He's blond with blue eyes, thin and fine-boned. Whereas I've never considered myself to be beautiful, my son is truly handsome. I might be biased, though.

When he puts me on my feet, I put a hand on each cheek. "How are you, baby boy?"

He grins. That's the one thing he got from his father, the same boyish grin that Benjamin used as a tool in his arsenal to charm women. On Tommy, it's not a tool, it's genuine.

"I'm great, Mom. Never better."

Kris joins us in the kitchen and kisses his husband, then says, "Mom has been in here all afternoon working her fingers to the bone."

"I have not!" I retort. "The menu for tonight was on the counter, so I did some prep work so it would be easy to put things together once you got home."

"Aw, Mom," Tommy says, "you didn't have to do that, but I'm glad you did. Let me go change and I'll be right back."

Tommy and I prepare his menu for the evening while Kris picks out complementary wines. When he was a boy, Tommy helped me in the kitchen all the time. He loved to cook and apparently still does.

Hours later, the guests have come and gone, the housewarming a hit with all their friends. The boys and I are in the living room enjoying a glass of wine before we clean up. Kris rises from where he's been snuggled up on the sofa with Tommy and goes toward his office.

When he returns, he's carrying the package I shipped here instead of putting it in storage. "I've been dying to see what's in here, but once he found out you were coming, he insisted on waiting for you to be here before he opened it."

"You didn't have to do that, honey," I say.

"I know," Tommy says. "I wanted to."

Tommy takes the small pry bar Kris brought along with the package and removes the boards protecting the cardboard box. Once he's got it opened up, he slides the painting out and gasps.

"Mom? Are you sure?"

"Absolutely. You always loved that painting, especially once I told you the story of how, during a trip to New York, my grandmother bought it from a struggling artist just a few years before he became famous."

He leans the canvas against the wall and steps back, Kris coming to his side. "Is that?" Kris whispers.

"Yes," Tommy confirms. "Mom, it's too much."

"I want you to have it. The paperwork is in an envelope taped to the side of the box. There are several pieces I will be re-homing; I've set aside the Seurat for Maggie, and, if I can ever get him to speak to me, the Bosch for Ben. Some I will sell, others I'll donate or loan out to be displayed."

"I always hated that Bosch one," Tommy says. "But all that scary, weird shit suits Ben. That thing used to give me nightmares."

I chuckle. My father loved that painting, but I never liked it either. That Tommy and Kris love the painting so much lets me know I've made the right decision.

"Maggie told me you were talking about downsizing," Tommy says.

I wonder what else she told him. She never could keep secrets, so she probably told him everything about the weekend of her graduation. However, her father's activities aren't exactly a secret. If he didn't want to be seen with his girlfriend, he shouldn't have taken her to Boston.

"Yes. It's just too much house for one person and I've never liked it, anyway."

"Good for you," Kris says.

"How's Dad taking it?" Tommy asks.

"Not well, but I don't care. Other than sleeping there a couple of nights a month when he's looking for money, he hasn't lived there for years."

"Why don't you divorce him?" Kris asks.

"I'm working on it. There are a lot of legal knots, but now that I know Maggie is staying in Boston, I have a new attorney focused on untangling them."

"Good," Tommy says and begins gathering up the packing materials to dispose of them, and Kris helps him.

With that as a signal that our break is over, I go to the kitchen to start putting food away and loading the dishwasher.

The next day, we roam all over Denver, shopping, laughing, eating, and drinking our way around town. Late in the afternoon, we end up in Boulder and meander around the Pearl Street Mall. If I were ever to move to Colorado, Boulder would be where I wanted to land.

However, I don't see myself leaving Oklahoma even though my children aren't there anymore. It's home for me. My friends are there and now that I have Ford in my life, perhaps we'll form those ties that bring us together for the long haul.

Thinking of him, when I go upstairs at the end of the day, I text him.

Me: *You still up?*

My phone rings and his name displays on the screen.

"Hi."

"Hey, Darlin. How's the visit going?"

"Wonderful. You sound tired and if you're just getting home, it's been a long day."

"It has been, but talking to you perks me right up."

I chuckle into the phone. "Somehow I think if you were to sit down, you'd fall asleep."

"You're probably right."

"I don't want to keep you. Mostly I was missing you and wanted to hear your voice."

"I'm glad you called because I've been missing you, too."

Surprising words come to mind, but instead of saying them, I simply say, "I'll let you know when my flight gets in tomorrow. Good night, Ford."

"Please do. Good night, Darlin. Sweet dreams."

The call disconnects, and I fall onto the bed. Did I really just almost say, "I love you" to Ford? Maybe it's just because I'm used to saying it to my kids or Monica and they're the ones I talk to most.

Surely I can't be falling in love with Ford already. We've only known each other for a few weeks. I've never been in love before, so I don't really have a measuring stick to go by. There's the love I have for my children and Monica and had for my mother, but that's not romantic love.

I thought I loved Benjamin, but I think most of my affection for him was grounded in a desire to get away from my father.

What I felt all those years ago can't even begin to compare to what I feel now.

But is this love? Does Ford have feelings for me, too? I don't know and I'm not going to stress about it. What's meant to be will be.

Chapter 28

Caitlyn

"Girl, we have got to talk," Sheryl says when she sits down for lunch on Tuesday.

"What's up?" I ask.

I'm hoping it's something about the house. There have been a couple of showings and the open house on Sunday, but I would think that if there had been an offer, she wouldn't have waited to tell me.

"I got some feedback on the showings from the other realtors and the weapons wall has to go," she says.

"What?" I say with a laugh. "It's not like it's staying with the house. I just haven't had a chance to pack it up and put it into storage." Dealing with my office was next on my list, but I guess I didn't get to it quickly enough.

"Well, you need to make it a priority. It's creeping people out."

That makes Monica laugh.

"What are you laughing about? This is all your fault!" I tell her since she's the one who gifted me with all those weapons.

It only makes her laugh harder.

"I'm sorry," Monica says when her tickled funny bone settles down, "but that is so silly. It's not like having a few pointy things means you go around using them on unsuspecting strangers. If you need help packing, let me know and I'll come help."

"I have already started boxing everything up," I tell Sheryl. "The office has been on my radar to take care of, but a few other things have taken priority."

"Yeah, like an asshole husband and a hot new boyfriend," Monica supplies.

"What boyfriend?" Francine asks.

I forgot she wasn't at our last lunch when we discussed Ford. Monica takes it upon herself to tell them all about meeting Ford and elaborating on every single detail of the meeting with Benjamin.

"I wish I could have filmed the whole thing," Monica says. "The expressions on Ben's face...oh my God, they were priceless!"

"Don't you think it was a little overboard for this Ford person to show off his gun like that?" Francine asks.

Rather than point out that Ford is a law enforcement officer and wasn't exactly showing off anything, I let it go.

"I don't," Sheryl says. "You missed seeing the shiner Ben gave her when he got mad about being cut off financially."

"You cut him off?" Francine sounds scandalized by the mere thought of me taking more control of the finances. Benjamin giving me a black eye didn't seem to bother her at all. That makes me wonder about her home life.

"I did," I say coolly. "I see no reason for me to keep supplementing his income when he has all but moved out and has a girlfriend who is seven months pregnant. She is not my responsibility."

"I'm not saying that she is," Francine replies. "It's just that you have so much, and it wasn't like it was hurting you financially to help him."

"Hurting me or not, I feel no obligation to subsidize his fucking around any longer."

Yes, it's a crass way to put it, but I don't care. How dare Francine presume to scold me about my handling of my family's money?

Francine sucks in a breath and looks at the other two women. Monica holds Francine's look, her face hard. When they don't jump to her aid, Francine stops speaking and focuses on eating her lunch.

I tell them about Ben calling me and accusing me of trying to cheat him.

"That asshole," Monica says. "I almost hope he doesn't divorce you, too. As much as I'd like to see you no longer tied to him, it would be poetic justice for his own idiocy to leave him with empty pockets."

"This cop you're dating is black?" Francine asks.

"Not that it matters or is any of your business, he is half black and half indigenous and he has been better to me in the short time we've been together than Benjamin ever was," I answer.

"Indigenous?" Sheryl asks.

"That's the PC way of saying he's Indian," Francine tells her. She probably thinks she's hiding it, but there's a curl of disgust to her lip.

"Indians are from India," Monica says, her voice rimed with ice. "Native American is a misnomer. People like me, who are from the native tribes of North America, are most appropriately addressed as indigenous. And again, not that it matters, but just in case inquiring minds want to know, my heritage is Cherokee, whereas Ford's heritage is Choctaw."

Francine levels a look at her. "I don't know why you're trying to make me out to be a bad person or some kind of racist."

"I'm not trying to make you out to be anything, Francine. You're doing that all on your own," Monica replies, unfazed.

Francine looks around the table. Sheryl abhors conflict and is intently focused on her plate. Monica hasn't looked away from her. I continue eating, unflustered by the conversation.

Francine takes her napkin from her lap and places it over her plate. She looks around for a server to get her check.

"Don't worry about it, Francine," I say. "I'll take care of it."

Her face goes stony, but she nods and rises to leave. No one tries to stop her. Sheryl bids her goodbye, but she's the only one. I have a feeling this is the last time our Tuesday lunch bunch gets together.

Based on today's comments, I'm not sad about that. It just goes to show that people will choose to reveal themselves in the strangest ways. I know Francine's view of life is quite superficial, but the shiny surface is apparently covering some pretty dark depths.

Monica stops our server and asks for a glass of the same wine I'm drinking. Determined to shine some sun on the dark cloud left in Francine's wake, I engage Sheryl.

"So anyway Sheryl, I'll let you know when I have the office cleared of weaponry. I will shoot for having it completed by the end of the weekend and if I can't get it done myself, I will hire someone to come get it taken care of."

She smiles at me. "That will be perfect. Once that's done, we'll look at setting up some more open house dates."

"Perfect. Were there any other notes you needed to pass along?" I ask.

"No. That's all."

The rest of the lunch passes with light conversation and laughter. Maybe we don't have to disband altogether but can continue our Tuesday lunches with a party of three.

Chapter 29

Caitlyn

The fitness center at the Society is amazing and the trainer I am working with is decent. After the first few minutes, I gave him some feedback on what I expected to receive from him, and he adjusted quickly.

For the first time in a long time, I'm breaking a sweat with my workout. Instead of having me just do the machines like my previous trainer did, he suggested a few different activities and I like them.

Who would have thought that wiggling a couple of ropes up and down would be such hard work? Another one that I felt to my bones was what he called sitting on a wall. With my back to the wall, I scooted down until my knees were bent and just stayed there until he called time. I can feel that they're working different muscles.

I'll probably be a little sore tomorrow, especially since it's been a few weeks since I worked out, but it will be worth it. Yes, all the way around, my decision to join the society has been a good one.

Once I'm showered, I go to the dining room to find one of my cohorts at a table.

"Serena! How are you?"

"Good evening, Cait. I am well, and you?"

"I'm great and glad you're here. We didn't have much of a chance to get to know each other at the orientation session."

She smiles shyly. "I know, and I apologize for that."

I reach over and put a hand on her arm, then chuckle. "No need for that. It was a bit of an overwhelming evening for me just trying to keep straight which hall went where."

She chuckles with me.

"You said you are relatively new to Oklahoma. Where did you move from and what brought you here?"

"I grew up in Louisiana and went to college and law school at Southern. Upon graduation, I was offered a position at a large firm in Atlanta. I worked hard and performed well. Before long, I made a bit of a name for myself, but my goal was to secure a judgeship. It's something I'd wanted since I was a girl."

"That's very impressive," I reply.

"Some view a legal career as too demanding, but I ate it up. I've always loved the law. There was a case over which I presided and the outcome wasn't what anyone expected. Some things happened, and I decided it was time for a change."

She takes a drink of her water. I can see that telling her story has ghosts walking behind her eyes, so I don't press for more. Thankfully, a distraction presents herself when Gabriella comes rushing in.

"I'm so sorry I'm late!" she says, dropping into a seat with a huff.

"You're not late," I insist. "We haven't even ordered yet."

"I don't know where my head is lately. A grand plan to get here early and work out was all set, but when I tried to find my bag with my workout clothes, it was nowhere to be found. Like a loon, instead of just grabbing different clothes, I spent way too much time looking for the bag I'd prepared."

"Did you ever find it?" Serena asks.

"Yes! It was right there under the table by the door below my purse. I guess I just overlooked it when I was first on my way out."

She grabs up a menu and reviews the daily specials quickly. That doesn't seem like something she'd do, but perhaps I don't know her as well as I think I do.

"Anyway," she says, with a grin. "I'm going to get something decadent for supper, since I'll be working it off afterward."

"I went to the fitness center today, and I have to say that I was pleasantly surprised. It's the first time I've worked out since I left my previous facility and I think I'm going to be feeling it tomorrow," I say.

We talk about the facility and the trainers for a while, but something about her misplaced bag is niggling at the back of my mind. It seems as if there's something I'm missing, but I just can't seem to put my finger on it.

As my mind whirs, I'm lost to the conversation. What is it I'm not seeing? "Cait?"

"What?" I ask, startled, then I see the server ready to take our order. "Oh, sorry."

I give the server my order, and once he's gone, Serena asks, "What were you thinking so hard about?"

My neck goes warm. Because I can't connect the dots in my mind, to say why I'm bothered by Gabriella's comment, I deflect. "Oh, I was just thinking about my boyfriend. We met at the gym I used to go to and I miss seeing him when I'm working out."

"Ooo...tell us all about him," Gabriella says.

Talking about Ford is easy. I tell them how we met and about him being a police officer. Again, that feeling that I'm missing something surfaces, but I can't figure out why.

"Anyway," I say finally, "enough about me. What are you working on this week, Gabriella?"

"It's a bear of a project, but I'm excited to get started on it. I just hope my construction crew can handle it. The scope is broader than they're used to working on. They're great with straightforward construction, but sometimes struggle with the decorative stuff and that seems to be the type of work people want me for."

"I can see how that would be," Serena says. "Artisans are difficult to find. My brother has a construction company, and he says that just getting reliable help is an issue, much less someone who has a lot of skill in the industry."

"Have you had any luck selling your house or finding a new one yet, Cait?" Gabriella asks.

That leads me to tell them all about the feedback I received from Sheryl and explaining the origins of the weapons wall.

Before the story is complete, they're both laughing and I've forgotten all about whatever it was I couldn't remember.

Chapter 30

Ford

I lead Cait through the club, focused on the back of my sister's head. I told her I might be able to make it tonight, but she'll be surprised that I've actually shown up. She will be even more surprised when she sees I brought Cait.

Thanks to Al and Bonnie, the entire family knows about her and I've told my sister, Adella, all about her. Adella has been hounding me to bring her over to Al's for a big family get together, but with Cait's trip to Denver last weekend, it didn't work out.

I'm not sure I'm ready to expose Cait to the entire family, but she's supposed to go to Al's with me tomorrow for lunch. If I don't get called into work today. The only reason I'm not worried about tonight is because I made it clear I was going to be in Tulsa and unavailable. It wasn't my turn to be on call, anyway.

I put a hand on Adella's shoulder. "Hey baby sister," I say, leaning down to speak in her ear. The band hasn't started, so it's not up to full volume in the club yet, but the music is loud enough to be distracting.

She clasps my hand and looks up at me. She then looks past me and sees Cait. Her face lights up and she stands, completely ignoring me now.

"You must be Cait!" she says, holding her arms out.

Cait grins back at her and steps into the hug. "I am. You're Adella, right?"

"Yes, ma'am! It's about time my brother got us together to meet."

"Since y'all don't need me to introduce you, I'm going to go to the bar. Darlin, you want something?"

"Just a beer is fine; you know what I like," Cait says, giving me her sweet smile.

"Dell, you need anything?"

"I'm good for the moment," my sister replies.

I lean down and kiss Cait on the cheek. "Be right back," I tell her.

She smiles and nods, then turns back to my sister. They're still standing, chattering away when I return. I knew they would hit it off. Both of them have big hearts and aren't afraid to show how much they care for those they love.

I give Cait her beer. "I'll just be over here," I tell her teasingly and sit down at the table, leaving a seat for her to sit next to my sister.

She puts a hand on my shoulder and remains standing, still talking to Dell. It seems that whenever we're close, she has to be touching me. I like that. I never thought of myself as a touchy-feely person, but with Cait, a lot of things I used to believe were true have changed.

Never, ever, did I think I'd even consider settling down again, much less getting married. Lately I find myself thinking about those kinds of things a lot. It worries me, though, about whether she's on the same page. She's just now disentangling herself from Benjamin and might not be ready to settle down again anytime soon.

The band begins moving onto the stage, getting ready to start their set. Cait takes her seat next to me, putting her hand on my thigh. I put my arm around her and tuck her close to my side.

She doesn't stay there long, though. Once the music starts, she's moving and wiggling in her chair in time to the music. Her face is beaming. She's obviously having fun and I'm glad to see it.

She leans over to me and puts her mouth close to my ear. "They're fantastic!"

I don't get a chance to answer before she has turned away toward the show again. As I'm watching Cait, I see my sister looking at me. When she catches my eye, she mouths *I like her* exaggeratedly so that I can tell what she's saying.

Me, too, I mouth back.

She rolls her eyes at me and goes back to watching her baby boy playing bass guitar on stage.

The band takes a break and my nephew, Jerome, comes to the table. He leans down to kiss his mama on the cheek. "Hey mom!"

I stand and shake his hand. "Hey, Uncle Ford. How are we doin'?"

"Great. You guys have really found your groove."

The boy pulls up a chair and sits to talk. We're lost in conversation when the house lights dim for a second, signaling the next set is about to start.

"Well, I'd better go," Jerome says. Then he lifts his chin to me. "Wanna come do one?"

"What?" Cait asks, looking wide-eyed between us.

"Go on, Ford," Dell says. "You know you want to."

She's right. I do. It's been a long time since I played in a club.

"All right," I say, and lean over to kiss Cait's cheek. "Be right back, Darlin'."

On stage, Jerome hands me his electric guitar that used to be mine, and takes the acoustic in hand as he leans into the microphone. "My Uncle Ford's in the house tonight and I asked him to come up for a song. He's the one who taught me how to play and put the music bug in my blood."

I turn to the other band members and tell them the song I'd like to do, and they all nod. When Jerome steps back from the mic, I tell him, and he grins.

As soon as I start with the very familiar riff, the crowd cheers. I'm not a talented singer, but on this song, I do alright. I chose it because I'm not so great with words a lot of the time, but thanks to a wordsmith like Clapton, it says what I feel about Cait, and I hope she gets the message.

When I look across the crowd at her, she's grinning from ear to ear and that brings out my own smile. I hold her eyes as I deliver the line I most want her to hear, and a few moments later, the song is done.

As I make my way back to our table, I'm patted on the back and congratulated, but there's only one person's opinion I care about. "You've still got it," Dell says and hugs me.

"Wow! That was amazing!" Cait says. "You didn't tell me you could have been a rock star!"

I laugh and pull her into a hug, then kiss her, pouring my heart into it.

"That was fun!" Cait says when we are settled in the car, headed home. "Thank you for taking me!"

I pull her hand up that I'm holding and kiss the back of it. "You are welcome, Darlin. I'm sorry it took me so long to take you out on a proper date.""Oh, Ford! I have enjoyed spending time with you, no matter where we are or what we're doing."

"I just feel bad that I haven't had a lot of time to take you out and show you off."

"Ford, I know your job is demanding and I am completely okay with that. I don't need someone to hold my hand and reassure me constantly. You come home to me when you can and let me take care of you and I'm content. If we get the time to go out and do something fun, that's just icing on an already delicious cake," she says.

I can hear the earnestness in her voice, and that settles my soul.

"I feared you might think I only wanted you for your cooking and sex," I say it in a joking tone, but it's honest.

She chuckles at that. "I'll admit that it has been nice to have someone to take care of again, but you have shown me in a hundred different small ways that you care about me, and it's more than sex and good food."

I nod. "Good. I do care about you, Cait. A lot. But I don't want to push you into anything. I mean, for Christ's sake, you're just getting out of your marriage, and I can't blame you if you're not ready to get into another."

She turns in her seat so she is facing me as best she can. When we stop at a red light, she says, "Ford, look at me."

I do.

"I have, for the most part, been single for over twenty years. The divorce might be just now getting processed, but I haven't been in a relationship for a long, long time. You are not pushing me. I am a very willing participant in everything that's going on between us."

A car honks behind us. The light has turned green.

"So, does that mean we're going steady?" I ask with a grin.

She barks out a laugh. "I suppose so. I'm not seeing anyone else, and I hardly see how you would have had time for someone else when, except for showering and changing clothes, you're with me when you're not working."

"There's no one else for me, Cait. Only you." I glance over at her, catching her eye. "Only you."

She smiles shyly at me and says, "Good. It's the same for me, Ford. There's only you."

She falls asleep on the way home. I hate to wake her because she looks so peaceful, but I stroke the back of my hand across her cheek when I park in her drive.

"Hey, Darlin. We're home."

She draws in a deep breath and shifts in her seat. When her eyes open and she sees me, her lips spread in a brilliant smile. She puts a hand to my cheek. "Hi."

I take her hand in mine. "Let's get you up to bed."

"Mmmkay."

The nap in the car must've given her a second wind because as soon as I settle into bed, spooned against her back, she turns to face me. Her soft lips trail kisses across my chest.

"Cait, what are you doing?"

"Nothing," she replies innocently.

With a press of her hands on my shoulders, she urges me onto my back and climbs on top, straddling me. I rest my hands on her thighs and let her do what she wants.

She is so beautiful, and it's amazing that she doesn't even realize it. Her hips move and she strokes my cock with her body. The folds of her sex part and her slickness coats my shaft as she moves back and forth.

God, it feels good. She looks down at me and smiles, all innocence. The woman knows damn good and well what she's doing to me and there's nothing about it that's innocent.

"You're torturing me on purpose, aren't you?" I ask in a rough voice, sure I can see devil's horns sprouting on her head.

She giggles. "Since when does torture feel so lovely?"

Leaning down, she kisses me as her hand slides between us and wraps around my cock. She shifts her hips down and back to take me slowly into her body, extorting a groan from me.

The little minx giggles again when she hears my groan, then sits up on top of me, undulating her hips. She pulls my hands up to her breasts, showing me what she wants.

How anyone could have thought she was frigid is beyond me. She is sex appeal personified as she moves her body in rhythm with mine. Her head drops back, her pale hair dangling down her back as she gives voice to a moan.

"I dreamed about this all the way home," she says. "Making love with you is better than I ever thought it could be."

Her hips move faster, and I match her tempo.

"Oh, that's nice! I used to think there was something wrong with me and then you come along with your roguish grin and big dick and lit me up like a Christmas tree."

"Darlin, I appreciate the compliment, but if you're going to talk while we do this, talk dirty."

She lets out a throaty laugh. "I said big dick. And your big dick feels so goddamn good that I'm about to come all over it. How's that?"

I laugh, bouncing her a little with it. Her mouth goes round and with a look of complete surprise, her body clenches around mine, squeezing me so tight I lose myself inside her.

This woman. She's causing me to lose myself in her in more ways than one. She has me in body, soul, and heart.

Chapter 31

Ford

Cait is fussing over what to wear, despite me telling her about a million times that she should just wear what she's comfortable in. What was supposed to be lunch at Al's has turned into a mini family reunion. Adella, Al's twin, is coming down from Tulsa, but Marnie and Juanita are also coming up from Dallas just for lunch.

It might be for lunch, but it's mostly to meet Cait. As soon as I agreed to bring her, the Pickering family hotline lit up like fireworks, calls and texts popping back and forth. I didn't realize me having a girlfriend was that big of a deal.

Part of me hopes I get called into work. I love my family, but all of them together are overwhelming, to say the least. However, my sisters and Bonnie would probably shoot me dead if I didn't show up after all this build-up.

"Darlin, you look beautiful. If we don't get going, we're going to be late."

"I could be wearing a garbage bag and you'd say the same thing," she replies with a huff. I can't help but grin at her because she's right.

"Yes, I would, because it would be true. You're beautiful no matter what you're wearing."

"I just want to make a good impression."

"Cait, you've probably never made a poor impression in your life. You're kind and loving to everyone you meet. My family is going to be crazy about you. Now, get a wiggle on or Bonnie's gonna chew me out for not showing up on time."

"Okay," she sighs. "I guess I'm ready."

I hope so.

On the drive over, I can tell she's nervous, so I reach over and take her hand in mine. There's a slight tremor in it, so I give her a squeeze of reassurance. She wants my family to like her and I have absolutely no doubt they will.

As soon as we walk into the backyard where Al is grilling, Cait appears completely unflustered and free of nerves. At least to anyone who doesn't know her. Adella spots her first and comes our way.

"Cait!" my sister exclaims and hugs Cait like they're old friends while the rest of the hen party watches on. You'd never know they just met a few hours ago.

Just as I thought would happen, Dell takes Cait by the hand and tries to steal her away from me. Before I let go, I ask her, "Darlin, do you want something to drink?"

She turns that beautiful smile on me. "Yes, please."

I pull her back to me and give her a peck for that smile. That smile tells me everything is right with the world and melts my heart. She's going to be just fine.

As soon as I take her a beer, I'm shooed away by the women-folk, so I join Al by the grill. "Where's the Texas faction?" I ask.

"In the house watching TV with the boys," he grumps.

He'd probably rather be in there, too. This whole shindig is disrupting his peaceful Sunday. With company other than me, it means he's unlikely to get his Sunday afternoon snooze in the recliner. Can't say as I blame him for being a little riled.

"Sorry," I say.

He shrugs and flips the burgers. "Glad you were able to come and I look forward to meeting your gal." With a quick glance to where the women are seated in the shade before he returns his attention back to the grill, he observes, "She's pretty. What's she doing with you?"

I know he's teasing, but I bump into him just enough to throw him off kilter. "She is, and I don't have a clue, but I'm just going with it until she comes to her senses."

It's a joke, but a part of me wonders if someday she might wake up, look over at me, and realize she can do better. That may happen, but for now, I'm just rolling with it. Cait is a one of a kind woman, so I'm not going to take a single moment for granted while she's mine.

Al starts putting burgers onto a platter and calls out to his wife, "Baby, burgers are done."

"Great!" she replies, then raises her voice so everyone can hear. "Come on, everybody, let's head into the house. I've got everything set up in there. Fix your plates and we can come back out here to eat where there's room. It's a gorgeous day, so we might as well enjoy it."

We're well into the meal when the first hitch in the road comes. Juanita's husband, Phillip, asks, "So, what is it you do for a living, Cait?"

Her money doesn't matter to me, but I don't want anyone getting the wrong idea about her. However, I shouldn't have worried. As usual, my girl handles it with ease.

"Mostly, I manage my family's trust," Cait answers. "My father sold the family business and set the funds into a trust. I handle the investments and such as well as sitting on the boards of a few non-profits."

Direct and concise, like it's no big deal. However, Phillip decides to be an ass, as usual. "Investments, huh? How much are we talking about?"

Cait starts to answer, but Adella, ever the protective older sister, jumps in. "Now, you wouldn't like me airing your annual salary to the family, would you, Phillip? How about you stop being rude?"

Yep, my sisters adore her if the glares on the women's faces turned toward Phillip are anything to go by. From the corner of my eye, I catch Cait smiling to herself as she looks down at her plate. I lean over and kiss her on the temple.

A few hours later, we're still sitting outside, bellies full, enjoying the day and the company, when my phone buzzes. Everyone groans. Sure enough, it's work.

"Well, I'm glad we got a few hours with y'all before the inevitable happened," Bonnie says. "Cait, we've loved having you over. You are welcome in our home anytime."

Cait hugs Bonnie. "Thank you so much for a wonderful meal."

From there, the mutual admiration society takes about twenty minutes saying goodbye before I get her out to the car. They don't seem to care much whether I'm there or not. Yeah, I'm exaggerating, but I knew they'd love her.

She's grinning when she buckles herself in.

"Your family is wonderful," she tells me.

"They think you're pretty wonderful, too."

Chapter 32

Caitlyn

My phone rings and I don't recognize the number, but I decide to answer, anyway. "Hello."

"Hi, Caitlyn, this is Heather. We met the other night. I was wondering if we could meet and talk."

"Heather? Benjamin's Heather?" I ask. She's the only Heather I recall meeting lately.

"Yes."

I have no idea why she could possibly want to meet. However, we are almost through Benjamin's deadline to sign the agreement, so maybe she wants to talk about that. "Sure. Would you like to come to the house?"

"No!" she says quickly. "Sorry, no, I think it would be best to meet somewhere that Ben wouldn't expect."

This is strange. I'll meet her somewhere neutral, but I'll also make sure it's public. She seemed to be so submissive to Benjamin that to call me like this if probably putting her at risk. I wonder what could have driven her to do it. There's only one way to find out.

"How about we meet in the food court at Quail Springs?"

"Yes, that will work."

We set up a time that works for both of us later today. Because it seems so unusual, I text Ford and let him know about the meeting. I'd rather someone know what's going on just in case something happens.

I doubt Heather intends to do anything, but Benjamin might, and she seems to be very much under his thumb. Ford texts me back, asking me to call him once the meeting is over.

I return to packing up the things in my office. This is the last room that needs to be addressed because I've been putting it off. However, even without Sheryl's admonition, it is becoming more urgent for me to remove anything I don't want to allow to be sold with the house.

The lead of Sheryl's that may have wanted the house lock, stock, and barrel didn't pan out, but interest in the house is ramping up now that the listing has gone live online and is widespread. Particularly since I asked that the listing make it clear that I'm willing to deal.

I head to the mall in plenty of time to meet Heather. My goal in arriving early is to scope things out, so to speak.

I have been trying to puzzle out why she would want to meet in private with me, but I don't have a clue. The only thing I can imagine is that perhaps Benjamin is going to use her to persuade me to give him more money. Knowing him, he probably thinks I won't be able to resist a pregnant girl's pleas.

I stand on the floor above the food court and look over the area. There are no signs of Benjamin, but I do see Heather already seated and waiting. This is so odd.

Might as well get it over with.

I circle around to the stairs on the opposite side of where Heather is seated, so I can get a good look at the areas I couldn't see from the floor above. Still no sign of Benjamin. I linger behind the elevator because I can see through to observe Heather. Neither Ben nor anyone else approaches her.

Feeling silly, I give up the surveillance and cross the court to where she's seated.

"Hi Heather," I say as I come close. She's looking the other way and jumps a little at my voice. Now I really am concerned. "Are you okay?" I ask.

"Sorry, I'm fine," she replies, but I can tell she's not.

"What's going on, Heather? Why did you want this meeting?"

She lets out a sardonic chuckle. "Right to the point it is." She sighs. "Something is wrong with Benjamin."

"Wrong?"

"Ever since that night at your house, he's been acting weird. He's angry and has a quick temper now. He's never had one before. Oh, don't get me wrong, he can throw a tantrum that would make a two-year-old jealous when something doesn't go his way, but it's usually a quick blow up and he's over it."

I nod. "Yes, he's had that problem for a while now."

He would get upset and bluster and blow and ten minutes later he would be over it. That's partly why I was so surprised by his lingering and growing animosity.

"It's like he's on drugs or something, but for the life of me, I don't know what he could be taking. I haven't seen him eating, drinking, smoking, or taking any pills outside of his usual blood pressure medicine and vitamins." She pauses. "Every day, the anger grows, and you seem to be the focus of it."

"Me?"

"He pitched a fit all the way home after that night we met at your house. He went on and on about how you were trying to screw him out of what's rightfully his. Since then, it has grown worse. He says your father screwed him out of what should have been his and now you are, and over the past few days, he's been ranting a lot and talking about doing violent things."

"Violent things?"

"He's talking about hurting you and your man. His name is Ford, right?"

I nod.

She goes on. "I'm not trying to scare you, but I wanted you to be aware. Last night, it was terrible. He kept hitting the wall. He did it so much one of his knuckles split open and he was leaving spots of blood everywhere he hit after that."

Across the food court, someone drops a tray and I think Heather barely stops herself from getting up and running.

She leans in and lowers her voice to a whisper.

"When I said something about bandaging his hand, he turned on me. The look on his face was...scary. I backed away from him and he...it was like I was prey and he wanted to hurt me. He swung at me, but I was turning away, so he caught me in the back. He hit me so hard I almost fell down. The only thing I could think of was that if I hadn't been turning away, he would have hit me in the stomach. He could have hurt the baby."

My hand goes to my mouth. "Oh, no!"

She nods. "I'm leaving to go to my mother's house in Kansas City as soon as I leave here. He will probably blame that on you, too. The way he's acting, I can't say if he'll try to do something to you or not, but I thought you should know."

"I appreciate you telling me, Heather. Is there anything you need that I can help with?"

She shakes her head. "I'm fine. My mom sent me some money for gas and stuff, so I don't have to use the credit card Ben gave me. He'll probably figure out where I'm going, but maybe it will slow him down enough so that I can get there and get settled with some of my family before he finds me. My mom can't stand him, so it won't be the first place he looks, but it will be in the top five."

"You have my number. If you need anything, let me know," I tell her.

"I'm gonna go," she says. "Take care, Caitlyn."

"Be safe, Heather."

Chapter 33

Caitlyn

I watch her walk away and go up the escalator as I think about everything she told me. She didn't give me the feeling that she might be lying, but I don't know her at all. If you combine today's conversation with the meeting she came to with Ben, I've spent under an hour with her.

I get up and leave the food court and make my way out of the mall. Once I'm closed in the car where there are no prying eyes or ears, I call Ford and relay the conversation to him. He takes so long to respond that I wonder if the call has dropped.

"I don't want you staying at your house alone any longer," he finally says. "I want you to pack at least enough for tonight and come stay at my house. Tomorrow should be a day off for me unless something comes up. We can get your office packed and into storage and talk about either moving you in with me or somewhere else if you don't want to come to my house."

"Do you really think it's that serious?"

"I don't know. She could be blowing it all out of proportion, but I'd rather be safe than sorry," he answers. "I don't want to risk you."

I've been to Ford's house, but I have never stayed all night there. He says that he prefers staying at my house in case he gets called out in the middle of the night so I can wake up in familiar surroundings.

I know he probably thinks that's what I want, too, but honestly, it really doesn't matter to me. Staying at his house is another step forward in our relationship.

It has only been a short time since that first day we spoke at the gym, but I know without a doubt that Ford is the kind of man I want to be with. He's the kind of man I deserve. He's not perfect, he works a lot and can get obsessed when he's working on a case, but I'm not the same woman I was when I got married.

I am used to being independent and handling things myself. If someone wanted to come in now and tried to be the kind of husband my father wanted me to have, I would laugh him out the door. Ford is someone with whom I can be a partner.

I will never despise him for his dedication to his job, just like he is supportive of, and actually seems to appreciate my independence. We can let each other be exactly who we are and intertwine our lives together into something new. He's everything I never realized I needed.

"I understand," I reply. "Me, too, better safe than sorry."

"Do you remember the gate code and where I put the key?" he asks.

"Yes, of course."

"Pack up and go over. I'll be off in a couple of hours and will see you there."

"Okay, Ford, I'll see you then."

"Love you, Darlin."

The call disconnects.

Wait a minute. Did I just hear what I think I heard?

I stare at my phone, but no message appears to clarify, so I put it away and start the car. Maybe he said it by mistake. We get used to saying the words when we're talking to family and friends and other people that we're familiar with.

Maybe that's all it was, just a slip of the tongue. I've caught myself saying it to people out of habit when it's not something I really meant for the person I was speaking with.

What if it wasn't? What if he meant it? Didn't I catch myself about to do the same thing a few days ago? I have powerful feelings for him, but love?

Can I even trust myself to know what love is? The last time I thought I was in love, I ended up with Benjamin and that has been a disaster. Not a total disaster because my three children came out of my union with Ben, and I wouldn't trade them for the world. Not even Ben Jr.

I gather everything I need from the house, including the stuff in the kitchen I intended to fix for dinner. At Ford's house, I unpack the groceries, but leave my overnight bag sitting by the front door. I don't want to make any assumptions about which room I'm sleeping in with it being the first night I sleep here. My nerves are getting the better of me and I don't like it.

It's weird being alone here. I kind of want to snoop, but I won't, at least not a lot. There's a little time before I need to start dinner, so I limit my snooping to looking at the photos of Ford's family that are everywhere.

In every single photo, the smiles are broad and genuine. My children haven't smiled like that in photos since they were little.

That thought makes me a little sad. I am not perfect. Not by a long shot, but I know I did the best I could to create a stable and loving home for my kids.

Feeling melancholy, I stop looking at the photos and go into the kitchen. I'll take my time fixing dinner. In Ford's refrigerator, I find the bottle of wine I left here the last time I visited. It doesn't look like he's touched it.

I notice the beer supply and see that he needs restocking. I smile to myself. The man likes what he likes and there's nothing wrong with that.

By the time Ford gets home, dinner is almost done and I'm on my third glass of wine. I'm feeling a little tipsy and I like it. I don't usually drink a lot, but the alcohol has settled my nerves and I'm feeling much more relaxed.

He comes into the kitchen to find me dancing to some music I put on. I spin and see him there, leaning against the doorframe and watching me, a grin on his face. He steps in and takes me in his arms, moving us to the music.

When the song ends, he leans down and kisses me. "Hey beautiful," he says when he pulls back. "Something smells in-credible."

I lean against him and nuzzle his neck. "Yes, it does."

"Mmm...wanna come take a shower with me?"

"I would like that. You go get started and I'll be there in a minute," I tell him.

He pats my butt. "Don't be long," he says as he starts pulling at his tie and turns to leave the room.

A thrill goes through me. I am still astonished that just a few months ago, I envisioned living the rest of my life alone, solitary, and sexless. Now I feel like I'm starting over as a teenager again and when Ford and I are together, I have a hard time keeping my hands off him.

I'm ravenous for him. I've never had sex in a shower before. This should be fun.

I step into the bathroom after ensuring that dinner stays warm but doesn't overcook, or heaven forbid, burn. Ford watches me through the glass door of the shower as I undress. The desire in his eyes thrills me and makes my skin tingle.

When I join him in the shower, the desire is showing in more than just his eyes. He's fisting his arousal, which is hard and heavy at the juncture of his thighs. My pulse kicks up and my core goes liquid.

I go to him, intent on replacing his hand with mine, but he turns me so I'm facing away from him. He pulls me back against him, pinning his erection between our bodies.

He nuzzles my neck, planting kisses along my shoulder, which makes me shiver. Rough hands reach around to fondle my breasts and tease my hard nipples.

I lay my head back against his shoulder, enjoying the sensations he's creating in my body. Reaching behind me, I grip his hips and press back against him. I moan when he pinches my nipples hard.

"Do you like that, Darlin?"

"Yes," I gasp.

One of his hands snakes down and cups my sex. I rock against his palm. He slips a finger between my lips to find me drenched.

"Mmm..." he says in my ear, his breath tickling. I shiver again, but it's a toss-up whether it is from his whispers or from the way his finger is stroking my clit so nicely.

I lean forward to brace myself against the wall and push my hips hard against him. He takes the hint and adjusts his position behind me. It only takes a breath before he's stroking the weeping head of his cock against my slit, making me moan louder.

I roll my hips. "Please," I say.

He grips my hip with one hand as he guides himself home with the other. I push back against him until he's fully seated. His sword fits my scabbard perfectly. I almost giggle at that thought because it reminds me of the wall of weapons I've been working on packing.

"I love your ass," Ford growls. "That first day in your house you were walking in front of me and all I could think of was pulling down your pants and having you just like this."

Ford rolls his hips, pressing even deeper. With his hands gripping my hips, he begins to move. Pumping his body against me, slower and steady at first, but he quickly picks up speed.

"Harder," I say.

He obliges and starts to piston in and out.

"Oh, yes, harder, Ford!"

He starts to pound my pussy with his cock. I am completely surprised when his hand smacks against my ass, but based on the "Yes!" that rips out of me, it's a pleasant surprise.

I hear him chuckle. He grips one shoulder and is thrusting into me so hard I feel like he's trying to drive his cock out the top of my head.

Smack!

"Ah!" I cry out. I start to tell him I'm close when he smacks me again and drives me over the cliff into freefall, causing my words to morph into unintelligible sounds.

He thrusts a few more times and, with one final hard pump, he finds his release. He stays buried to the hilt for several long moments, and I can feel his cock throbbing. I don't know how long we stood there, joined and absorbing the pleasure as it courses through us, but he milks himself with a couple of strokes, then pulls out.

We clean up in the cooling water of the shower then get dressed to go out to dinner. The first time we made love, Ford was very gentle, very careful. I appreciate that, but as time has gone on, we've progressed into more and more adventurous territory.

I know it might be quite, what's it called...oh, vanilla to some people. However, considering the fact that while I was married, the only sex we had was in the darkened confines of our bedroom in the missionary position, it's all new to me. And I like it. I like it a lot.

I like oral sex. When I dress sexily and see how it turns him on, it thrills me. I enjoy having sex all over the house. And I really like being on top. When he smacked my ass in the shower, I loved that.

If you had asked me before it happened whether I thought I'd like it, I probably would have said no. Who knew spanking was a turn on? There is a whole wide world of things to try, and I'd like to try as many as Ford is open to. I think maybe I'd like to try tying each other up next.

"I liked that," I tell him. Unless I communicate about what I like and don't like or that I'm willing to try new things, he might be wondering or being cautious.

"I did, too," he says.

"What do you think about bondage? Maybe tying one another to the headboard?"

He chokes on the bite he was swallowing and coughs. A swig of beer clears his throat, and he looks sideways at me. "What did you say?"

I shrug, feeling my neck grow hot. "I was just thinking that there are a lot of things I haven't tried. Spanking didn't seem like it would be a turn on, but it was, so I'm wondering what else I might like."

He chuckles. "Darlin', you never cease to surprise me."

"That's a good thing, right?" I ask, suddenly unsure.

He shows me his boyish grin. "Absolutely."

Chapter 34

Caitlyn

"I'm taking this to the dining room. Another box done and ready to go," Ford says, lifting the box and leaving the room. "Great! Just four thousand more to go!" I call after him.

I can hear his laugh echo back to me. He comes back to the room and asks, "How on earth are we supposed to pack a spear?"

We're in my office surrounded by boxes and bubble wrap and weapons. Most of the easier items are packed and in the dining room ready to be moved to storage. We have the bulkier and trickier items left.

I look up from the Damascus blade. It's so beautiful that I took it out of its sheath to admire it before I wrap it in plastic and paper. I set it next to its sheath on the corner of the desk and look across the room to Ford, where he has the bronze spear in hand as if he's ready to run into battle.

"Maybe we don't need to pack it," I say. "It's made of brass, so maybe just wrap it in a cloth and stand it in a corner of the storage? I don't think it needs to be put into a box."

"Agreed," he says.

"There are some old sheets in the closet next to the bathroom you used the first night you were here. We can use one or two of those and secure it with tape or twine or something. The sheets are old enough that if they need to be thrown away afterward, it won't be a big deal."

"I'll go grab a couple," he says and heads back out the door.

"I got three in case one isn't enough. We can wrap them round and it will give some cushion," he says as he enters the room. He puts his hand on the spear to drape a sheet over it when there is a loud pop followed by a clicking noise.

"What?" I say, confused. Ford's entire body is gripped in a rigid spasm as if he's having a seizure, then he falls forward, taking the spear with him.

"Ford!" I scream and race across the room to him.

Motion in the hallway catches my eye. Benjamin stalks toward me. "Where is she?" he grits out.

"Where is who, Benjamin?" I ask, standing.

"Don't fucking play innocent with me, bitch. I know you convinced her to leave me. I know you're helping her because she doesn't have any money. It's not enough that you have ruined everything else. You had to take her away, too."

His eyes are wild and crazy. The man's face is crimson. His clothes are rumpled and disheveled. He looks unhinged.

"Are you talking about Heather?" I ask.

His hand flies out and backhands me across the cheek. I put a palm to the burning mark and start to back away from him.

He doesn't just look unhinged; he is unhinged. A maniacal laugh comes out of his mouth, making my blood turn cold.

"Now you're going to take me seriously because if you don't tell me what I want to know, I'll beat the shit out of you until you do."

"Benjamin, I don't know where Heather is. I haven't seen her since she was here with you."

There's no way I'm going to tell him what I know and unleash him on her. Ford's been hit with a stun gun, and I don't know how long it will take him to recover, but the effects can't last forever. Unless the jolt of electricity gave him a heart attack or something.

Fear swamps me. Ford could be lying there dying and there's nothing I can do about it. No, he's fine, I tell myself. He has to be.

My back hits the desk. I start to move left to try to get around him. Benjamin punches me in the stomach, knocking the air out of me.

Although he's already hit me once, I was still doubting he would hit me again. I've got to stop thinking of him in the way he used to be. This violent version of Ben is the new normal, and I have to behave accordingly.

I double over as all the air leaves my lungs, and he grabs my hair, pulling until I straighten. "Not so tough now that the boyfriend isn't able to save you, huh? Where is she?"

"Ben, I..."

He grabs my shoulders, yanks me forward, and shakes me until my teeth rattle. Then shoves me hard back against the desk. The pain radiating up and down my spine takes my breath away just as I was regaining it, and I fall to the floor. He pulls me up by my hair again and hits me in the side.

I don't go all the way down again, but only because of the grip he has on my hair.

"Ben, please..."

My words are cut off by the Mack truck that crashes into the side of my head. Everything goes black.

I come back, unsure how long it has been, but Ford is still prone on the other side of the office, so it can't have been very long. Benjamin is shaking me and ranting.

"I told you. I told you. Tell me where she is. Tell me now. I know you know."

When he sees I'm conscious again, he puts both hands around my throat. I panic and start to claw at his hands and his forearms, trying to create even the smallest gap that will let me get a breath.

He squeezes harder and lifts me, slamming my back onto the desk. He leans over me, the position allowing him to put all of his strength into choking me.

I kick. I flail. I can't get leverage to land a blow or throw him off balance.

Nothing is helping, but I will keep fighting as long as I can. Black spots begin to fill the little bit of vision I have left. My hands scrabble across the desk, finding nothing.

Just as everything starts to dim, my hand closes around something hard. My brain is too oxygen deprived to decipher what it is, but it's hard, so I bring it up and slam it into Ben's side with all the strength I can muster.

He grunts and squeezes harder. I pull back and slam the item at him again. His grip loosens a bit as he grunts again, but it's too late. Everything goes black, as I think how terrible it will be for my children to know their father has murdered me.

Strange shapes are looming over me. I put my hands up to block them, but gentle hands move my arms back down to my sides. I can't see clearly, but I can hear Ford's voice. "It's okay Darlin, these are friends. Be still and let them work."

I try to speak, but it sends fire through my throat. I'm scared and I don't know what's happening and I can't speak. Hot tears sting my eyes and start to pour down the sides of my face. My throat swells, which makes it hurt even more than trying to speak did. I start to shake.

A firm hand grips mine. "Shhh...Darlin." Ford croons. "Just relax."

I squeeze his hand hard, but I can feel panic starting to surge through me. The shaking worsens. I have no idea what's happening.

I can't breathe! I can't see!

"Mrs. Foster, we need you to calm down." It's a stranger's voice, so that makes it worse instead of better. "Jerry," the voice says.

I feel a prick in my arm and after a few moments, I start to fade back into blackness.

Wakefulness comes slowly. I try to turn my head but can't. My neck feels like it's wrapped in about a million winter scarfs, claustrophobic and itchy.

I reach up and touch...something. When I try to speak, nothing comes out. Instead, it hurts.

A lot of things hurt. My neck hurts. My throat, my head and face hurt. I stop cataloging when I realize it would be easier to list the areas that don't hurt.

I still can't see very well. I still can't talk. From the sound of beeping machines, I can tell that I'm likely in the hospital. At least I'm alive.

I try to find the call button for the nurse. My hands are frantically feeling around for buttons on the bed. Strong hands wrap around mine.

"Hey Darlin, it's okay. You're fine."I relax at hearing Ford's voice. My head won't turn when I try to look his way. The bed moves as if he's sitting on it, but I can't see him.

I can't. I can't. I. I can't see him.

I can't breathe. I can't see. I can't breathe. Oh God! I claw at whatever it is around my neck, but I can't get it loose. I'm trying to gulp in air, but none of it will go past my throat.

"I need someone in room three-forty. She just woke up, and she's having a panic attack. She can't breathe," Ford says.

There is a flurry of movement, and everything goes black again.

Chapter 35

Caitlyn

When I wake again, I can see a little more clearly, but I still can't move my head.

"Hello?" I croak out in a whisper.

There's no answer. I feel around on the bed and find the television remote. I hold it up where I can see it and am happy to see there's a call button on it. A nurse answers.

"Hello?" I say. I want to say more and be more cordial about it, but that's all I can manage to get out.

A few minutes later, a nurse comes in. "Mrs. Foster, it's good to see you awake." She starts taking my vitals, which frustrates me. I want to know what's going on and I want everyone to stop calling me Mrs. Foster when Mr. Foster just tried to kill me.

I pull my arm away from her when she tries to take my blood pressure. She looks at me with a frown. I point to whatever it is around my neck and hold out my hands as if asking what.

She doesn't get it and tries to take my arm again. I yank it away again and hold out my hand and use my other to mimic writing.

"If you'll let me take your blood pressure, I'll get you something to write with," she says.

I move my head up and down the millimeter that whatever is around my neck allows. She finishes logging the test results and leaves the room.

It takes her so long to come back that I think she's not going to. I sit up and try to move around on the bed to the edge when I realize I have a catheter.

Damn.

I sit back. Frustrated because I have no idea what's going on. I don't know what's wrong with me or where anyone is.

For all I know, Benjamin's here in the same hospital with me, but I don't know what hospital I'm in. I don't even know what goddamn day it is.

The urge to scream is strong, but I can't. I can't even manage to cuss out loud.

I shove the tray table that's by my bed. It goes rolling away and crashes into the wall on the other side of the room, spilling the pitcher of water that's on it. I'll probably feel bad about that in a few minutes, but right now, it feels pretty darn good.

"Well, someone's in a tiff," Ford says from where he's standing in the doorway.

I scowl at him. His face softens.

"I'm glad to see it," he says.

I scowl at him again, and he laughs. In two long strides, he crosses the room. He takes me in his arms and squeezes me gently. I'm surprised that he's shaking.

After a dozen long breaths, he loosens his hold and leans back to look at me. He smooths my hair back behind my ears.

"They kept you out for a couple of days until the swelling in your face went down so you'd be able to see. There's a lot of damage to your throat and it will take a while longer to heal, so your ability to speak will take time to recover."

I try to reach up to feel my face, but Ford catches my hands and pulls them down.

"You don't want to do that, Darlin. Benjamin really did a number on you."

I have a million questions but can't ask them. My hands slide inside his jacket and start searching his pockets.

Ford tries to stop me, but I won't be deterred. I finally find what I'm looking for. I pull out his notepad and pen.

What happened? I scribble.

"Well, you're going to know more about that than I do. Benjamin came into the house and hit me with a stun gun. I went down and hit my head on that damn spear. Apparently, he attacked you and you fought back. I came to and found both of you on the floor in front of your desk. You weren't breathing, so I did CPR until the EMTs arrived. You came to and panicked, so they knocked you back out and brought you here."

Where's here? I write.

"You're at Mercy," he answers.

Where's Ben?

He doesn't answer. I underline the words with three bold lines.

"He's dead, Darlin."

I frown. Surely, I haven't heard him right. I look at him.

He nods. "It looks like in the struggle you grabbed the dagger and stabbed him while he was choking you."

My last thoughts before I blacked out during the struggle come back to me, but instead of it being Benjamin killing me, I'll have to tell my children that I killed their father.

Oh God, I killed their father. Sorrow swamps me, but I'm surprised when it's not for Ben. I am filled with sorrow for my children.

Need to call kids.

"I've already talked to Thomas and Margaret. I left a message for Benjamin Jr., but haven't heard back from him yet," Ford tells me.

My tear-filled eyes find his. I wonder if he told them.

"I only gave them broad strokes," he says, reading my mind. "I told them that there was an accident, that you are hurt, and their father is deceased." He takes out his handkerchief and wipes away my tears.

There's a knock at the door. I look up to see two men standing there. "Come on in guys," he says, then looks at me. "These are the detectives working the case. They'll have some questions for you. Do you think you're okay to answer?"

I nod. He dabs the remainder of my tears away.

Need something else to write on. Use notebook up.

"I'll get you a bigger notepad," he says and rises from the bed. "I'll be right back, guys. She's still not able to talk much, but she can write."

I stare at my hands, trying not to cry anymore. The detectives introduce themselves, but their names float by in the ether.

"Mrs. Foster, we'd like to go over the events of Saturday evening. When Ford gets back, would you please write down what happened? I'm going to read you your rights."

I give another millimeter nod. He goes through the listing of my rights and asks me if I understand. Although it's just a croak, I manage to give an affirmative because he needs more than a head nod.

This probably isn't anything that could be used against me anyway, because I'm sure I'm on pain meds. I have nothing to hide, but I'm not stupid, either.

Ford comes back in with a letter size note pad and another pen. I give him his notepad and pen back with a shy smile. Taking the notepad from him, I begin to write. I can feel Ford reading over my shoulder.

Call attorney, Andrea Hartmann. Ask her to come or send someone from firm.

Ford calls her for me. She's not a criminal defense attorney, but they should have someone on staff who can come and advise me. I have no doubt that everything will be found to be self-defense, but I'd still rather have counsel on hand.

Thankfully, she's available and says she'll come right away. True to her word, it only takes about thirty minutes before she comes striding through the door with Simon and another woman in tow. She hands cards to the three men.

"I'm Andrea Hartmann," she says, "this is Paige Whitman and my assistant Simon Jones."

The detectives fill them in on the situation and that they'd like for me to write what happened with Benjamin at the house. She tells me to write it down, so I do.

Benjamin came in. We didn't hear. He zapped Ford. Ford fell. Ben mad about Heather, his pregnant girlfriend.

I wouldn't tell where she'd gone. He hit me. He shoved me into desk. Hurt my back. I fell.

Pulled me up by hair. Hit me more. Hit me in side of head. Blacked out.

Came to. Choking me. Tried to fight. Scratched him. Tried to find something on desk. Found something hard. Hit him with it two, maybe three times. Passed out. Woke up. Freaked out. EMT knocked me out with a shot. Woke up in hospital.

I hand the notepad to the attorneys. They read it. Paige nods at Andrea and hands it to the detectives. They read it and look at Ford. "This corroborates what you said and fills in the blanks."

"What did you say?" Paige asks Ford.

"I said what she said up to the point where I got tazed and hit my head. When I came to, Cait and Benjamin were on the floor in front of her desk. She wasn't breathing, so I called it in and started CPR and did it until the EMTs arrived."

"Detectives, I think you have everything you need for now. I'd like to confer with my client," Paige tells them.

"We'll probably need to talk with her again, but there's nothing pressing," says one detective. He hands the attorneys his card, then he and his partner leave.

Both women look at Ford. "That includes you, Detective Pickering."

I shake my head as much as I can but when I realize they aren't looking at me, I write *NO!* in big letters followed by *He stays.* I hold up the notepad and wave it at them.

"Who are you to her and why does she want you to stay?" Paige asks him.

"I'm her boyfriend," Ford says.

Both women look at me.

"She can't really speak right now, so I can answer most of your questions. Our relationship is fairly new. We started talking around the time of her first meeting with you, Ms. Hartmann."

He goes on to tell them about Benjamin's threats and the meeting with him and Heather and gave them Monica's name as a witness to the meeting. He relayed what I'd told him about the meeting with Heather and what she'd said about Benjamin.

"I had her stay at my house the night before the attack and we spent Saturday at her house packing up her office to prepare for the sale of the house. Then Benjamin showed up. You should know, the hard item she thought she hit him with was actually a very sharp and pointy blade. She stabbed him twice with it. The autopsy shows that one of the blows made it up under his ribs and nicked his heart. The other sliced through his liver."

I nod as best I can and write on the notepad. *That, along w/the notes the detectives took is all of it. Ford - Tox screen? Ben acting weird.*

"I'll ask if they did a drug screen with the autopsy," Ford says.

"I doubt they'll see this as anything but self-defense." Paige adds. "I'll stay on top of it and will be in touch with you."

"Thank you," I croak.

Paige winces. "You just focus on getting better. Let me worry about the legal stuff."

The three legal eagles say their goodbyes and leave the room. Exhaustion swamps me as I sag back onto my pillows.

"You are wiped out, aren't you, Darlin?" Ford asks with a tender look on his face.

"Yes," I whisper, then wince.

"You're not supposed to talk, Cait. They want you to keep the cervical collar on for the time being."

He sits on the bed and faces me, reaching out to smooth my hair. If I've been knocked out for a few days, I'm sure I stink to high heaven and my hair is probably disgustingly greasy.

Feel gross. Probably look grosser. I write on the pad.

"You look alive and that makes you the best kind of beautiful," he tells me. "I know you're tired, so get some sleep. The doctor said he would be down in a couple of hours. I'm going to go check in at the office and I'll be back."

I mouth okay without saying it. He kisses my forehead and leaves.

When he's gone, I let myself cry, even though I probably shouldn't. It makes my throat and eyes swell, but it uses up the last ounce of my energy and I'm soon unconscious again.

Chapter 36

Caitlyn

Voices rouse me from a deep sleep.

"Who are you, and why are you the one who called me? And why are you just waltzing into the room like you belong here?" someone hisses.

I open my eyes to see my daughter's back squared as she faces off with someone. My position on the bed blocks my view, so I find the television controller and bang it on the side rail of my bed.

Maggie swings around. "Mom!"

Once she moves, I can see that it's Ford she was talking to.

"Hey, Darlin," Ford says. "Sorry we woke you."

He moves around Maggie and comes to my bedside, where he takes my hand and kisses the back of it.

"Darlin?" Maggie says, mocking Ford's Oklahoma drawl, and she takes in his movements.

Ford looks her in the eye. "My name is Ford Pickering. Your mother and I met at the gym we both went to and struck up a friendship. Over the course of recent weeks, it has grown to more than that."

Maggie looks between the two of us. I reach for my pad of paper and pen on the tray table.

It's true. I write and show it to her. *He called you for me. I can't speak. Throat damaged.*

"Will someone please tell me what happened?" Maggie asks.

He looks at me and I nod as best I can. He squeezes my hand.

"You might want to sit down," he tells Maggie.

She sits in the chair next to my bed and Ford perches next to me. I reach out my hand for hers as Ford begins to tell her everything, starting with me deciding to list the house for sale. He ends by telling her again that her father is dead, but now she knows that I'm the one who killed him.

I dare a glance at her. The look on her face is a mixture of shock and horror. I loose her hand and write on my pad.

I'm so sorry.

She doesn't respond. Ford squeezes my hand. Of all my children, I know that Ben's death will hit Maggie the hardest.

Benjamin didn't have much use for his sons. Ben Jr. was too much like his father, selfish and manipulative, for them to bond. Once Tommy came out as gay, Ben wanted nothing to do with him.

However, he doted on Maggie. She and I are close, but our relationship was nothing like hers with her father.

The moment is broken by the doctor's appearance. Maggie gets up and goes into the bathroom. I'm not surprised that she needs a minute to take it all in.

The doctor doesn't tell me anything I don't already know. I have damage to my neck and throat. I need to keep wearing the cervical collar for a while longer, but everything is healing nicely, and should return to normal in time.

My spine doesn't appear to be damaged, but I have a lot of contusions that will also take some time to heal. He says that they want to keep me one more night and that if everything still looks good, they'll discharge me in the morning.

I sigh with relief. The doctor leaves and I see Maggie hovering in the bathroom doorway. She heard everything.

"Will they let her go back to our house?" she asks Ford. "I mean, is it blocked off as a crime scene or anything like that?"

"They may not want anyone in the office, but the rest of the house should be fine. Do you want to go back to your house?" he asks me.

"What do you mean by that?" Maggie asks, a little incensed. "Where else would she go?"

Ford levels a look at her. "She could go to my house if she doesn't want to go back to hers after her husband tried to murder her there. It might be a bit much for her."

I want to stop this, but I can't. They're both facing off again and ignoring me.

"But she's not the one who was murdered, was she?" Maggie spits out.

Ford raises an eyebrow. His voice is hard and cold when he speaks.

"Your father is the one who attacked *her*. *He* cheated on *her* for years, even brought his pregnant mistress to the meeting where your mom offered a peaceful ending to their marriage. She even offered him half the money from the sale of the house, although she didn't owe him a dime."

I hate it that I can't speak and stop this. Ford rises from his perch on the bed and levels a stare at Maggie as he goes on.

"But that wasn't good enough for him. He snuck into the house. Incapacitated me with a stun gun, then proceeded to beat the shit out of her. When she wouldn't give up the location of his pregnant mistress to save herself, your father choked her out. In her last moments, she landed a lucky blow. Then she died."

He steps toward her, and I can see that he's shaking. "She. Died. And if I hadn't come around in time to do CPR, she'd still be dead. Is that what you would have preferred, that she was dead instead of your father?"

"No!" Maggie exclaims. "Of course not!"

"Then stop acting like it," he snarls. He scrubs his face. "Listen, I'm sorry to be so harsh, but it's been a couple of long days of worrying if she's going to be okay. I understand it is a shock and I am truly sorry for the loss of your dad, but all your mom did was defend herself and I, for one, am glad she did. I wish no one had died; but wishing can't change the facts."

"Ain't that the truth?" a voice sounds from the doorway.

Surprised, I look up to see Tommy standing there with his Kris close behind. He grins at me. "Hi Mom. You look terrible."

I can't help but grin back at him. The pain makes me wince. He quickly comes to me with Kris on his heels. "I don't know who this guy is, but I like him."

My boyfriend. Ford. I write.

"Well, hello, boyfriend Ford. I'm Thomas and this is my husband, Kristopher."

Ford shakes their hands and hovers nearby when Tommy and Kris perch on the bed, one on each side of me.

"I think I'm going to go," Maggie says. "It was an early flight to get here and I just…" She doesn't finish as she gathers up her things.

Stay at house?

"Mom wants to know if you'll be staying at the house," Tommy conveys.

"Your room is ready if you want to stay there," Ford tells her. "Everything has been cleaned and aired out. If you do go there, stay out of your mom's office. I'll double check, but for now, it's best to treat it as a crime scene until I can verify that it's been cleared."

She narrows her eyes at Ford. "How do you know so much?"

"I'm a homicide detective with OKCPD," he tells her. "I'm obviously not investigating what happened with your mom and dad, but I still know what questions to ask and of whom."

"I don't know," Maggie looks at me and replies to my question. "If I decide to stay in a hotel, I'll let you know where I end up."

Thank you. I love you. I write and show it to her.

She nods and leaves.

"Bitch," Tommy says under his breath when she's out of earshot.

I smack him on the leg and frown at him.

"I'm sorry, mom, but it's true and Ford was right about how she was acting."

How much did you hear?

"We heard everything from him asking you if you wanted to stay at his house," Tommy tells me. He cups my cheek with his palm. "We're glad you're going to be okay. I don't know what I'd do without you."

I lean into his hand and cover it with mine. Oh, how I have missed my baby boy.

Tell me what's new with you and Kris.

Tommy and Kris fill me in on everything that's happened in their lives since I last saw them a few weeks ago. Much of it I already know from our regular conversations, but Tommy is in entertainment mode. He is trying to lighten the mood by metaphorically dancing in the spotlight to keep from lingering on what's in the shadows.

Chapter 37

Caitlyn

I arrive at home without a lot of pomp and circumstance, thankfully. Ford was the only one at the hospital when I was discharged. I figured the boys were sleeping in after driving down from Denver and I'm sure Maggie is still assimilating everything.

I decided to go to my house instead of Ford's to at least try it. The boys told me they'd be staying there, and I wanted to spend as much time with them as possible.

I had my fingers crossed that Maggie would be there, too, but I wouldn't be surprised if she had decided to stay at a hotel. I still haven't heard anything from Ben Jr. and that worries me.

Tommy is cooking breakfast when I shuffle into the kitchen while Kris and Maggie watch on while drinking coffee. Maggie's eyes are puffy from crying. I know she's grieving for her father and I can't hold that against her.

Maggie looks up and sees me. "Mom! You're home!" She comes and takes the arm that doesn't have Ford attached to it. "Where are we going?"

"She thought the downstairs bedroom would be best for now. She doesn't think she's ready for the stairs yet," Ford answers.

"Good idea," says Kris.

"If you'll take her the rest of the way in, I'm going to go upstairs and get her some clothes to change into. She hasn't showered since Saturday and is starting to stink," he teases.

I swat at his arm.

"You're the one who said it, not me," Ford says with a grin. "But it's true."

Tommy comes to replace Ford on my other side as if I'm some kind of invalid unable to move under my own power. I can't move quickly, but I can still get around on my own. However, I let them fuss over me without complaint.

Ford gets to the bedroom just after us and lays the clothes on the bed, then comes to me, undoing the Velcro on the cervical collar. "If you'll excuse us," he says to the kids.

They both gasp when the collar is removed. "Oh my God," says Tommy. "Is all that from…"

"Yes," Ford says.

I don't know what they see, but I can imagine the bruising is severe based upon my hazy memory of Ben's hands around my throat.

"I'll go start the water to let it warm if you'll start helping her undress," Ford tells Maggie.

"That's my cue," Tommy says and leaves the bedroom, closing the door behind him.

I unbutton my shirt. I was glad when Ford brought me one that didn't need to be pulled over my head because the muscles in my back are still very tender. I try to move it off my shoulders, but Maggie sees me struggling and pulls it off.

"Oh God, mom," she says when she sees the bruising that Ford tells me covers my back from my shoulders to the top of my hips.

I have no idea what I look like. I haven't seen myself in a mirror since the attack. She pulls my pants down and helps me step out of them. I'm standing there in just my underwear when Ford returns, wearing nothing but a towel wrapped around his waist.

"I'll take it from here," he tells Maggie.

He's looking at her over my shoulder and I don't know what passes between them, but after a few heartbeats, he gives her a nod. Maggie leaves and the bedroom door clicks shut when she closes it.

Ford removes my underwear and takes me by the hand. "Come on, Darlin."

He tries to keep me from looking in the full-length mirror that is leaning on the wall of the bedroom near the bathroom door. When I refuse to move until he gets out of the way, he sighs and shifts away.

I want to sob when I see myself. My face is a swollen mess. My neck is black and purple from all the bruising. I have bruises on my sides stretching from the damage on my back.

"It looks bad, but it's all going to heal and be fine," Ford consoles. "I love you, Darlin, and nothing is going to change that, not even a few bruises."

He leads me away from the mirror and into the bathroom. Ford steps under the warm water with me where he gently washes my hair and conditions it. With a light touch, he washes me from head to toe while I brace myself with hands on the walls.

Once I'm dried and moisturized, he helps me into clean clothes. The shower wears me out so much that I let Ford put me to bed.

I wake up sometime later to find Maggie curled up in bed with me. Poor girl. I know she's having a hard time.

When I try to roll over, it hurts so badly that I almost cry out. I can't call out for help either. In different circumstances, I would just stay put until someone comes along or Maggie wakes up, but my bladder is telling me that wouldn't be a good idea.

I reach out and shake Maggie. She wakes and helps me into the bathroom, waiting while I relieve myself.

"I'm so sorry, Mom," she says, her voice low.

It's unclear why she's apologizing and I don't have my pad of paper, so I just give her a small smile to let her know I heard her. When I'm finished, I manage to get my pants up on my own, but it exhausts me.

Instead of going back to bed, though, I want to see the men in my life and find my only means of communication. Maggie takes me by the arm and walks with me out of the bedroom.

The boys are still in the kitchen, or maybe back in the kitchen where Tommy is cooking again. I'm unsure of what time it is, but it's dark outside, so it must be supper time.

"Ford had to go to work," Tommy says when he sees me.

Waving a hand at the barstools, Maggie changes trajectory with me. When I perch on the stool, Kris puts my notepad and pen in front of me and Maggie takes the seat on the other side.

What's for dinner?

"We are having Chicken Piccata, salad, and garlic bread. You are having a smoothie because the doctor said no solid food for you for a few days while the swelling in your throat is going down."

Being the mature woman I am, I stick my tongue out at him.

Chapter 38

Ford

M y phone buzzes and I want to throw it against the wall. Of all the times to get called into work, today is not ideal. I'd said I was taking vacation so I could be available to help Cait.

There's only one reason why they'd be calling. "Pickering," I answer.

"Ford, it's Jim," my partner says. "I hate to bother you, but figured if I didn't call, you'd rip me a new one. We've got another dead girl staged in her home."

"You're right. You know I want this guy. Text me the details and I'll meet you there."

I disconnect the call and look up to see Tommy and Kris watching me. "I've got to go into work," I tell them. "There's been a murder and they need me to work the scene."

"Is it the Mannekiller?" asks Tommy. "Mom told us you've been working the serial case."

"I can't say," I tell them, "but I can say that it would take something like that to pull me away from your mom right now. She'll probably sleep for a while. When she wakes, will you please let her know what's happened?"

"Sure," Tommy says.

I pull out my wallet and take out a couple of my cards, handing them to the two men. "Here's my contact information. If anything happens with your mom, call me right away, if you don't mind."

"Okay," Tommy says. "She'll be fine, though. We'll take care of her while you're gone."

"Thanks," I say to both of them, meaning it more than the simple word could ever convey.

I arrive on the scene after a detour to my house to put on a suit. Everything points to this being the same perp as the other serial murders, but we'll have to process all the evidence to be sure. Bridget Vaughn is tied to one of the chairs at her dining room table, dressed to impress a potential date with a glass of liquid in front of her.

Just like the others, it looks as if she's sitting at a bar waiting for a date while having her favorite drink. I'm sure her age will be somewhere between twenty-five and thirty-five.

She'll be single and at least moderately successful. The perp has good taste in women, but it also means that he has to be the type of man who can catch their attention.

I think we should call in the FBI shrinks, but so far, the powers that be don't agree. Maybe Bridget will change their minds since she's the fifth victim of this psycho and we're still no closer to catching him than we were with number one.

Worry for Cait has me distracted, so I'm having a hard time focusing on the details of the crime scene. I let Jim take the lead when we go to question the victim's friend who found her. They live close and work at the same place, so they rideshare, trading off who drives to work each week.

When Bridget didn't come out, the friend texted to alert Bridget of her arrival. After a few minutes, a call was placed and went unanswered, so the friend got out and knocked on the door, then moved on to peeking in windows when she saw Bridget sitting at the table, definitely not dressed for work.

The police were called and upon arrival made entry into the home and soon after called for a team of detectives. My mind wanders as Jim talks to the friend.

There's not much she's going to be able to tell us beyond the discovery. She says they are work friends, but not really close outside of that.

I wonder if Cait's awake yet. I worry about how this is going to affect her relationship with Maggie. The girl was all but outright blaming her mother for getting attacked, and it made me want to shake her until her teeth rattled.

I'm still not over the fact that she died and that if I had started CPR a minute or two later than I did, she would still be dead. I can't get that out of my head. I came a hair's breadth of losing her forever when we're just getting started.

I had pretty much resigned myself to being a bachelor for the rest of my life and I had no idea that my passing appreciation of Cait would turn out the way it has. I lived a lot of years without her, but I can't imagine a future without her in it.

"You got anything else you want to ask?" Jim asks me.

I shake my head. "I think you covered everything."

We finish up with the crime scene techs and leave. "You gonna get your head in the game?" Jim asks. "You were all but useless in there."

"I'm sorry, man. It's hitting me hard that I came close to losing Cait."

"You're really that close to her?"

"Yeah, I am. I love her."

I assure myself that Cait is safe with her family, and I focus on working the case.

"Go over what the friend said."

He fills me in on the way back to the office. I'm making mental notes as he talks and compiling a list of all the things we need to do. Although I'm still not convinced it's going to yield anything, we'll need to pull her phone records.

The crime scene crew will grab her laptop and electronics to be reviewed. So far, there's nothing that leads me to believe the perp is someone the women knew beforehand.

My gut is telling me he's a stranger who stalks them and gets to know everything about them without them having a clue. How he selects them is a mystery, though. That's something I need to work on since the other avenues haven't panned out.

There has to be something we're missing, and that is one of the worst feelings a detective can have.

Chapter 39

Caitlyn

I'm settled into a recliner in the family room, feeling much better now that I've showered, slept and eaten. Kris brings me my laptop when I motion for it.

I can type much faster than I can write. The great thing is that it was on the kitchen table where I'd had it shopping for real estate instead of in the office as it usually is.

Once the kids are seated and comfortable, I start to type. Kris has pulled up a chair next to me and reads what I type out loud.

"She says you all will need to plan your father's funeral. She has the information for the place that did her father's funeral, but considering it was over twenty years ago, it doesn't really matter, so you can choose whomever you want. She also says you may want to contact Heather and include her in the planning."

Maggie frowns. "Who's Heather?"

"She is the woman you saw your father with in Boston. He has been mostly living with her for going on two years, except for the couple of nights a month when he would occupy a bed here. In another few weeks, she's going to give birth to your half brother or sister," Kris relays.

"What the actual fuck?" Tommy asks. "Why would we include her?"

"Because she loves your father," Kris says, reading it from my screen. "None of this is her fault, and she deserves to have her say in mourning him."

"Didn't you love him, too, mom? What about your say?" Maggie asks.

"Baby girl, remember what I told you in Boston. The last time I loved your father was the day you were born because he gave me you. But I hardened my heart against him a long time ago because I couldn't keep letting him break it over and over," Kris reads for me.

They argue, but I convince them to at least meet her. Maggie will be stubborn, but as much as he didn't get along with his father, Tommy is someone who brings people together.

He naturally sees what people need and helps them get it. It's what makes him so good at his job in marketing. He'll bring the women together and he does.

Heather has come back to town and comes over to meet two of Benjamin's children. She has a few things she wants to include, but mostly gives way to whatever the kids want. Some requests are significantly more than anything I would have done, but I won't stand in the way of however they want to memorialize him.

Over the next few days, I write check after check to finance my dead husband's memorial. Maggie and Tommy try many times to get in touch with Ben Jr. to see if he wants to have a say in what happens at the funeral, but he maintains radio silence. They finally give up and Maggie emails him the details.

It's Saturday and we're all dressed in our most somber clothes. I'm still very sore, worse in some places than others. The swelling in my face has gone down, but the bruises left behind there and the rest of my body are turning technicolor as they heal.

I have on so much makeup that I feel as if I'm wearing a mask and will don dark glasses for the service. However, I'm thankful for the chilly day that will make the turtleneck sweater bearable.

I don't need to be the focus of today. Today is for my children to memorialize their father's passing. Although my relationship, or really, lack thereof, with Ben was all but an open secret and many might criticize me attending his funeral, we were still legally married, and I will be there for my children.

I am changing purses when a card falls to the bed. It's the message from the fortune teller machine at The Belladonna Society.

The question you ponder, the answer you'll find, when the story you've started begins to unwind.

I remember my wish and I have to put a hand to the bedpost to steady myself.

I wish my husband were dead.

Those are the words I uttered that day when I faced the genie in a mechanical cage. Did I cause this? Is it possible that my wish set this all in motion? Is it possible that a machine can grant wishes?

"You all right, Darlin?" Ford asks. I haven't seen him much since he got called out. He had hoped to take some time off to be with me this week, but the serial killer has struck again and requires his attention.

I know some women might be hurt or angry at his dedication to his job, but I, for one, am thankful for it. Because of him, and other men and women like him, our city is safer and I will not ever try to make him feel bad about it. I'm sure that once the funeral is over, he will go back to working on the case, but he's here when I most need him and that's what matters to me.

I pick the card up and slide it into my purse. It's crazy to think those words have come true, but a sense of uneasiness sparks in my belly.

"Yes," I answer. My voice is returning, but it still sounds like I'm whispering most of the time. "I just lost my balance for a moment. I'll have to get used to wearing real shoes again."

"You can wear your house shoes if you want. I don't care what anyone thinks, and neither should you," he tells me. "But if you insist on wearing them, I'll stick close and be your leaning post."

I turn into him as he takes me into his arms. "How did I get so lucky?" I ask him.

He kisses me on the top of my head. "Aww, Darlin, I'm the lucky one."

The memorial service at the church passes without incident. Heather rides with us in the family car to the graveside service.

Maggie's mouth is flat with disapproval when Heather steps into the car. She looks at me and when I raise an eyebrow in response, she turns away to look out the window.

Ben Jr. shows for the graveside service, but he stands on the side opposite the rest of the family. I look at him, but there is no reaction. Like me, he is wearing dark shades against the sunny day, and I can't tell if he's looking back at me or not.

There aren't many mourners present. Heather is the only one of us clustered together as family that sheds a tear. The small crowd makes me glad I decided against having an additional reception at home. I think all of us are ready to have it over and done.

True to his word, Ford is a stalwart leaning post, supporting me physically as well as emotionally. The cool morning is turning warmer as we creep toward afternoon and standing for so long is tiring me quickly.

When I lean against him, Ford removes his hand from mine and puts his arm around me, which helps to relieve some of the pressure on my back. It's only then I realize I am shaking.

As soon as the service ends, Ben Jr. turns to leave. Tommy tries to catch his brother, but Ben is moving too quickly and has too much of a lead. He gets into a sedan that looks like a rental and leaves just before Tommy reaches the car.

"Asshole," I hear Maggie say under her breath as she watches the scene.

"Did you really expect anything else?" Kris replies, equally as quietly.

We linger for a short time, speaking with the other attendees and allowing them to give their condolences. Once we have spoken with everyone, we make our way back to the funeral home's cars to be returned to our personal vehicles at their facility.

"Heather," I say, "will you be staying in Oklahoma City?"

I realized this morning that I hadn't talked with her at all about her plans. She was living in the City when she and Ben got together, but it sounds like her immediate and extended family are in Kansas City.

She had worked with Ben and with him gone, I'm not sure she will want to stay with the company. I have no inkling of her financial situation, but with Ben being so desperate for money, I have a feeling it's not good.

She shrugs. "I'm not sure," she says. "I'll stay here until the baby is born. It's so close and my obstetrician is here, but after that, I don't know."

I had been thinking about giving her the money promised to Ben if he divorced me and, in that moment, I made up my mind to do it. Her child is Ben's child and should be taken care of. It is not my responsibility to take care of it for life, but two million dollars could manage a good life for the child and his or her mother if Heather didn't go crazy and blow it all.

I also decide that since I'll be giving away two million dollars to one child, it is only right that Ben's other children get the same amount. I will talk to my accountant on Monday and see how it would best be handled to minimize the tax impact on the funds. It would be a shame to hand over a large sum of money to each of them, only to have Uncle Sam take most of it away from them.

"Wake up, Darlin," Ford says as he gently shakes me awake. "We've got to move you to the other car to get you home, then you can take a nap."

I am overwhelmed with emotion. It has been such a short time since Ford stepped into my life and now, I can't imagine what I would do without him. Not to mention that I'd likely be dead if he hadn't been there when Benjamin attacked me.

Ford's solid presence has been my safe place through all this craziness. Although the demands of his job mean he might not always be physically present, his emotional support is always there. He has cared for me and seen me through the darkest days of my life across these past few weeks.

To many, we might seem like an odd match, the Detective and the socialite, but we work together. If someone had tried to fix us up on a blind date, I'm sure both of us would have said there's no way we could be a match. However, those first chance encounters provided enough of an enticement to have us wanting to know more, to dig deeper than the surface.

Having been independent for most of my life, I don't mind that he has a demanding job. When he is available to me, he is there, body, mind, and spirit. In turn, I am able to care for him and help protect that body, mind, and spirit from becoming too jaded by the evil he's exposed to every day.

I hope I bring some light and beauty to help beat back the dark. I don't know where life will take us, but one thing I know for sure is that wherever we go, I want to go together.

Shifting my position, I pull back and look up at him. I want to be looking him in the eye when I say it. "I love you, Ford Pickering. Outside of my children, I didn't know it was possible to love someone this much, but I do."

"I love you, too, Darlin. I love you, too."

Get a **FREE** copy of an expanded prologue that picks up where we leave Noémie in her apartment and follows her through the creation of the Society.
https://dl.bookfunnel.com/vrbyja0808

If you enjoyed A Pointed End, do me a solid and leave a review! It's not a book report; it's okay to keep it short. Have fun! Be honest!
https://mybook.to/PointedKitMcKenna
Thank you loves!
XOXO
Kit

About the Author

K it McKenna writes romance books with a slice of danger, blended with strong, seasoned women, and steamed to perfection set against the backdrop of Oklahoma.

Kit is a born and raised Oklahoma gal who has lived here her whole life except for a brief detour to hang out in the mountains for four years. She is an artist and free spirit who loves roaming around in the woods and finds great joy in the unusually and sometimes darkly beautiful. Kit has worn a lot of hats in her life, a server, a factory worker, nightclub manager, office administrator, state drone, and business owner.

A bit of a dichotomy, she loves all things positivity and light, but still loves to play in the dark. Her favorite book offerings range from authors like Eckhart Tolle to Stephen King. Her favorite movies are horror and holiday is Samhain (Halloween) but she still loves a good romance. She's a huge sucker for a story where the underdog comes out on top.

If the bar doesn't have a good cider, she'll opt for a fine whisky.

She comes to writing later in life after tiring of reading books that seem to only focus on perfect, perky, barely legal heroines.

Her stories are about real people who have their own demons, drama, and challenges to overcome.

You can find her on online at:

Website – www.kitmckenna.com

Facebook – @authorkitmckenna

Instagram - @kitmckennaauthor

TikTok – @kitmckennaauthor